THE MAN IN THE WOODS

ROSEMARY WELLS

The MAN IN THE WOODS

DIAL BOOKS FOR YOUNG READERS

E. P. Dutton, Inc. NEW YORK

Y

Grateful acknowledgment is made to the following for their help:

Dr. Raymond E. Phillips, Ross University School of Medicine
Professor Catherine Clinton, Department of History,
 Harvard University
Peggy Medeiros, New Bedford Preservation Society, W.H.A.L.E.
Dr. Nicholas Hodnett, Director Lab Research,
 Westchester Medical Center
Regina Deschere, Director Public Relations,
 Smith-Corona Corporation.

Published by Dial Books for Young Readers
A Division of E. P. Dutton, Inc.
2 Park Avenue
New York, New York 10016
Published simultaneously in Canada
by Fitzhenry & Whiteside Limited, Toronto

Design by Susan Lu
Printed in the U.S.A.
First Edition
COBE
10 9 8 7 6 5 4 3 2 1

Wells, Rosemary. The man in the woods.
Summary: Fourteen-year-old Helen investigates what she
considers the false arrest of a classmate, and is terrified
by death threats, which no adult will take seriously.
[1. Mystery and detective stories.] I. Title.
PZ7.W46843Man 1984 [Fic] 83-23958
ISBN 0-8037-0071-7

To Shelly, the silver fox.

THE MAN IN THE WOODS

ONE

First thing in the morning on the second day of school Helen Curragh placed five heavy textbooks, her binder, and the rest of her belongings on the shelf of locker number 1123. Unfortunately she closed the door and snapped the padlock shut before she'd tried out the combination. She squinted at the little tag which had been wired to the lock.

Memorize this combination: 34 left – 56 right – 3.
Do not tell any other student your combination.
Any student who tampers with another student's lock is subject to suspension.

C. Casey, Asst. Prin.

Helen spun the dial and tried the numbers. The lock did not open. She tried the opposite direction. The lock didn't open. She tried it three more times before banging it, but the lock just dangled from its chrome hasp.

Miss Podell, her homeroom teacher, had since vanished inside the classroom. Helen breathed deeply to drive away despair. All the other students around her were experimenting with their lockers, but none had been as rash as she. Helen yanked on the lock with both hands and all her strength.

"What's the matter?" asked a sandy-haired boy who was passing by in the hall.

"It won't open," said Helen.

"Lemme see," he said and gave her a helpless-girl look that Helen hated.

"What's the combination? Lemme see the tag on your lock."

"I'm not supposed to tell," Helen answered. "The tag says—"

"Aw, forget that," said the boy. "I won't steal your gym suit." He began twirling the dial.

Helen stood first on one foot, then on the other. This boy was so snippy she wished he would fail miserably. On the other hand positively everything she needed for the whole day was in the locker. She supposed it was all right that he was tampering with her lock. She stared at the back of his head. He didn't look as if he'd rob her locker. His hair was cut short and lay flat except for a cowlick smack in the middle. This morning's newspaper headlines suddenly occurred to her. "WHO IS THIS TEEN THUG?" the New Bedford *Post-Dispatch* had asked. The boy at her locker certainly looked nothing like what the paper had dubbed the "Punk Rock Thrower." The face in the police drawing resembled the Neanderthal man—or was it the Piltdown man?—in her science book. The Punk Rock Thrower had for some time been standing on the lonely hillsides around New Bedford, hurling rocks at passing cars. So far the police had no idea who it was.

"Can't get it," said the sandy-haired boy. "Must have the wrong tag on your lock."

Helen looked imploringly at him despite herself. "But my books, my notebook, my lunch, my sneakers . . . everything's in there," she said.

The boy only shrugged. "Welcome to the real world," he said and picked up his books and loped down the hall.

Helen pounded on her locker. It was one of the hundreds that lined every corridor in the school. It had queer little vents, top and bottom, as if to prevent the suffocation of a small animal were it to be put inside. Helen faced a day of explanations.

She wished she were back home in her warm bed. She wished she were back at St. Theresa's, where her books had been kept unlocked in an old-fashioned desk with an inkwell hole, and she didn't have to run to a different classroom every forty-five minutes. Why was this happening to her? Why did New Bedford Regional have to offer a better education than St. Theresa's High School? Last year her father had been quite convincing: St. Theresa's with its well-meaning nuns could not afford even a decent lab or art room. It didn't hold a candle to the regular high school, and Helen would never get into a good college with a second-rate parochial-school education behind her.

At the time the decision to go to the big high school seemed exciting. There was little left at St. Theresa's for her anyway. Her best and closest friend, Jenny Calhoun, had moved away to Houston, Texas. Tiny pricklings bothered Helen's eyes. She missed Jenny. Horribly.

As each minute went by, masses of students moved faster and faster in both directions past her. Four minutes were allotted between class bells. Four minutes to dash from the old building to the new. Four minutes to charge, dry-throated, up or down a jam-packed stairway. English was Helen's first class. She dared not be late and started to run. Where would the office be in this enormous school? Would anybody even be interested in her unopened locker? She felt completely naked without her books. She felt completely Saturdayish without her St. Theresa's uniform.

"You mean you put your books in your locker *before* you tried out the combination?" Helen was asked by her teachers all morning long. Each time she had to admit this was true. She knew that even if she got straight A's until June, every teacher in the school would think of her as an imbecile for the rest of the year.

During the morning she had collected several pieces of mismatched notepaper, borrowed hastily, on which she'd written, with a borrowed pencil, notes, homework assignments, and things to be remembered for ever and ever. Because her schedule with classroom locations was pasted on the inside cover of her locked-away binder, she was also late to all her classes and by lunchtime had been forced to describe her dilemma in front of a fully seated class three times.

While the other girls dressed for gym, the gym teacher placed an angry-looking check mark next to Helen's name in a Naugahyde ledger. Helen was advised that three checks meant failure in gym for the semester. She was then directed to find the janitor in the basement of the old building in the hope he could open her padlock.

Helen wandered, ducking under fat, echoing heating pipes and dodging around boilers, through a maze of passageways. In a paper cup she found a dead cigar butt that might have belonged to a janitor, but the owner was nowhere to be found. One of the dim, slug-brown hallways ended at a lighted door. The school crest and the word *Whaler* were painted on the frosted pane in red. Pleasant sounds of busyness leaked through the door, but Helen was afraid to open it. Instead she trudged up a flight of stairs, fighting off an overwhelming yearning to escape the school and run all the way home.

"Hall pass, please," a girl snapped at her as she emerged from the stairwell.

"I haven't got one," said Helen to the flat oval face over the badge that said *Hall Proctor.* "The gym teacher says they haven't been printed up yet for the year." Helen clutched the assorted bits of notepaper close to her chest.

"You'll have to report to the office then," said the hall proctor.

"The office!" Helen gasped. "I've been looking for the office all day! You see, I locked all my stuff in my locker, and I can't get it open. Even my lunch and my lunch money," she added thoughtfully, eyeing a bag of M&M's on the proctor's table. The oval face with the thin lips and the tiny eyes followed her gaze. The M&M's were emptied out onto an open math book on the table. "Only the dark-brown ones," instructed the proctor. "You a freshman?" she asked.

Helen picked out all five dark-brown ones. "Yes," she answered.

"The office is on the third floor of the new building, west wing. Go down this hall, through the breezeway, turn left, up three flights, turn right, right again, and there it is. It's funny," she said to Helen's fleeing back. "You look young even to be a freshman."

Helen talked to God as she raced down the hall. *Why am I so stupid?* she asked. *Why do I have to look so young? Please, dear God, why do I have to weigh only eighty-one pounds, and why did you give me such hideous naturally curly hair?*

When Helen was four years old, her mother died, leaving her and her father with Aunt Stella. Helen could barely remember her mother now, but she still dreamed about her and imagined she was around in difficult moments. She prayed to God nightly that in His compassion He would compensate her for being half an orphan. Helen wished that first of all, as a sort of coming-of-age present, God would straighten her hair. Then, if in a period of about three to six weeks he could slowly fill out her 28AAA bra to perhaps a 32A, she would feel normal at last. That wasn't asking much. Still, Helen knew He had no intention of doing these things because, as Sister Ignatius Paul had explained to her, she had already been handsomely compensated for the balance of her life by her extraordinary ability to draw, and everything had already been settled.

Helen found the office. A woman behind a window who looked as if she had a headache asked Helen for her hall pass. Helen said she had none. The brisk, pained voice directed her to another office across the hall.

"It's about my locker!" said Helen to the suddenly closed window. "The combination on the tag was wrong, and I locked all my things in it!" She heard her own voice rise squeakily.

"Get a pass from Mr. Casey first," answered the disembodied voice.

Wearily Helen pushed open the door across the hallway.

Clement Casey, discipline officer and assistant principal, stood with one leg resting on a chair, lion-tamer fashion. Across from him, slouching and stuffed into a first-grader-sized desk was Stubby Atlas. Helen recognized Stubby instantly. He was several years older than she, but there had been no end of whispering about him at St. Theresa's because his father was supposed to be a racketeer. Stubby had been kicked out for doing something unmentionable. Even Jujube Nelson, Stubby's best friend, wouldn't tell the rest of St. Theresa's what it was.

Mr. Casey, rosy cheeked and immaculate, a full head shorter than Stubby, looked at Helen in astonishment. "Are you in some sort of trouble?" he asked.

"It's my locker," said Helen. She bit down on her lip. "I locked all my things in it, and it won't open. The tag—"

"Across the hall," said Mr. Casey. "They handle that across the hall."

"But they sent me to you," she answered, her voice beginning to squeak again.

Mr. Casey opened the door wide. "Roberta!" he yelled

in a voice much bigger than himself. "Help this girl out, and don't send anyone else to me for anything short of murder! You hear?"

Behind Mr. Casey's back Stubby had removed a piece of costume jewelry from the pocket of his leather jacket. It was a string of beads that looked something like amber with an eagle attached to it. He swung it around his head like a bola. Helen looked at Stubby's face. His eyes were leering slits, set in pulpy, acne-scarred cheeks. It was not a face to forget.

"Gimme that!" said Mr. Casey. He snatched the chain away.

"It's my motha's!" said Stubby, winking evilly at Helen.

"I'll bet it's your mother's," Mr. Casey growled. "You either ripped it off some poor old lady on the way to school, or you stole it out of one of Perry and Crowe's trucks this summer. You had a job loading them, didn't you? You just slipped it out of a package, didn't you?"

Stubby slumped back away from Mr. Casey's jutting jaw. "I never stole nothing from those trucks," he said with an amused smile at the ceiling. "Ask Mr. Perry. Ask him."

"You got kicked out of St. Theresa's, didn't you?" Mr. Casey went on in a furious voice. "I got a letter about you from Sister Luke, Mother Luke, whatever her name is, over there. She warned me about you. You're into drugs too, aren't you, Atlas? Well, I'll tell you something. . . ."

Helen escaped the room. The last she saw of Stubby, he was still staring at the ceiling with an untroubled grin on his face.

"What's your locker number?" asked Roberta in a stale tone through her window.

"Locker number?" Helen asked.

"There are over three thousand lockers in this school," came the bored reply. "Each one has a number on a little plate. What's yours?"

"I ... don't know."

"Better find out." The window closed. The bell rang. Helen had no time to run back and find her locker number. *History,* she reminded herself. Because she loved it, at least for this class she felt prepared.

The history teacher, Mr. Brzostoski, was considered an oddball. That, Helen had concluded the day before from the amount of puzzlement in the classroom. The first thing he had said was that Brzostoski was too long a name to say and that everyone should call him Mr. Bro. The second was that the textbook was dull as dishwater and he would use it only as much as he had to. These openers had made everyone suspicious but hopeful that he might be easy. He dashed this hope by saying he expected every student to think and not just memorize and that he intended to be very tough. This had thrown the whole class into a silent tailspin.

Helen liked him. When she arrived at his class late, he didn't ask her why. He was eating a banana and simply nodded to her and gave her a thin blue essay book. He asked her to write everything she knew about the American Revolution.

The rest of the class was already sweating over this assignment. Helen took a seat in the back and began to write. The American Revolution, like the many historical events where England had been in the wrong, was a favorite subject of her father's. His buttery Irish brogue, which he turned on and off at will, rang in her ears. She filled six pages easily. Then on a blank sheet at the back she began to draw.

Helen was good at hiding the drawings she made in her notebook. None of the teachers at St. Theresa's had really minded her doing this. Helen was the school artist and had been since she could remember. Still, she didn't like hurting their feelings and pretended always to be taking voluminous notes while she was really caricaturing the teachers and her classmates or drawing political cartoons, which she saved for the delight of her father.

For eight years the nuns had asked the same simple artwork for every season of the year. Leaf tracings in October, turkey cutouts at Thanksgiving, angels at Christmas. Helen's turkeys were always distinguishable from the rest in the row that hung above the blackboard. There was always great expression in the eyes, and she usually added something extra, like a Pilgrim being devoured by his own turkey. Her angels dove athletically across St. Theresa's windowpanes in December, and one Easter she had done a large poster showing a mass of frightened chicks and rabbits pursued by a savage band of children. She had titled this "We Celebrate Our Lord's Resurrection by Torturing Innocent Animals for Profit!"

One day Sister Ignatius Paul had sat her down and shown her a certain page in the Sunday school book.

"What do you think of that, Helen?" she had asked.

On the page was an enormous hand, its wrist disappearing into a cumulus cloud above. In the hand were jewels, and the jewels dripped down to a bunch of miniature people, snatching at them from below.

"In olden times," Sister Ignatius read aloud to Helen, "jewels and money were called *talents*. Nowadays Our Lord gives us gifts, or talents, when He wants us to carry out His work in a special way.

"What do you think of that?" asked Sister Ignatius, as if she'd hidden jelly beans up the sleeve of her habit as a surprise reward for the right answer.

"The thumb is drawn wrong," Helen had observed seriously, and she had redrawn the hand properly on another piece of paper. It was then that Sister Ignatius told her that God had given her a special gift, a great gift, and she must use it to glorify His name. Sister had added that it was possible that God had chosen Helen because her mother had died. This part was unclear to Helen, as she could draw extraordinarily well even before her mother had taken sick, but she supposed that God had known about the shape of things to come ahead of time.

Mr. Brzostoski had eaten three bananas during the course of the class. Helen was so hungry she could barely look at them. She could have eaten a banana skin. The bell rang, and slitting the drawing out of the blue book, Helen passed in her composition with everyone else.

"Wait a minute!" said Mr. Brzostoski. He caught hold of her arm as she passed his desk. "That too!" he said and tweaked the drawing out of her hands. He looked at it for just a second and then said, "Come see me after school, please."

Helen stood in the doorway. The history class pushed

by her on its way out. The homeroom class was piling in. "Out of the way!" yelled someone, and she followed a pink Shetland sweater miserably back to Miss Podell's room.

Why did I have to do that! she yelled at herself inside her head. It was a bad start to her favorite subject. It was a bad finish to a terrible day, but, then, terrible days always snowballed themselves into disasters at the end, and today had been of the worst kind. She hoped against hope that Mr. Brzostoski would not look at the drawing too closely. She prayed that if he happened to be a right-wing Republican who hated Democrats such as her father, he wouldn't hold the drawing against her for the rest of the year.

The frosted pink sweater bobbed down the stairway. Helen rushed to follow it back to her homeroom and her lost, sealed locker.

Why didn't I at least draw a fashion model or a Swiss chalet on a mountainside? she asked herself. Helen had never in her life drawn either of these things, but they were popular subjects among the girls in art class.

The girl in the Shetland sweater was seated next to Helen in homeroom. A few minutes before the bell rang she tapped Helen's left arm politely. She wanted the attention of the girl sitting on Helen's right. *Glad to help,* thought Helen, patting the second girl on the sleeve. She watched them. *Oh, what I'd give,* she calculated, *to have gleaming blond, feathered hair like that. Such blue eyes too.* The girl in the pink sweater was the type who blushed easily when boys said things and always joked that she was on a diet when it wasn't true because boys stared at that kind of graceful, well-groomed, well-filled-out sort of girl. Instinctively Helen tried to flatten out the curly hair that grew obstinately out instead of down from her head. She cursed Aunt Stella silently for giving her bangs. Aunt Stella didn't understand curly hair. She had thought bangs would be the solution to Helen's problem, but when they were cut, they just curled themselves into a frizzy sausage on her forehead. If Helen could never hope to look like the girl in the pink Shetland sweater, well, at least just maybe she could be friends with her.

Across Helen's desk the two girls shared a whispered confidence, both of them leaning in toward Helen. Helen listened, wide-eyed, as if the conversation were the most important she'd heard in her life.

"Let's go down to the *Whaler* office after school and pick up our booster tags," said the blonde.

"Great!" answered the other girl, who was dark and equally pretty and grown-up–looking. Helen felt included. After all, they were both planting their elbows on her desk. She was about to ask what booster tags were and if she could come along with them when Miss Podell's ruler smacked a book on the front desk like a gunshot.

"This class will not be dismissed until I get sixty seconds of silence!" Miss Podell announced, looking daggers at Helen.

The girls on either side of her melted back into their seats giggling. They looked at each other, not at Helen.

She squeezed her eyes shut until the bell. She thought of Jenny Calhoun again. Houston was two thousand miles away. *You'll make new friends!* said Aunt Stella in Helen's mind. *Start with a friendly smile, and in no time you'll forget all your worries!* Aunt Stella made new friends every time she went to the beauty parlor. She did not understand how hard it was. What right did Helen have to hope these two old friends would want her tagging along anyway? Luckily she hadn't embarrassed herself by asking to be included. Besides, Helen told herself, she should have known better. One look had convinced her that these two girls would one day be cheerleaders or baton twirlers. They would have boyfriends soon, if they didn't already.

In the old days, a hundred years ago, she'd learned over and over in school, poor people waited hand and foot on rich people. They tipped their hats and licked the boots of the wealthy. Rich people with servants and mansions hardly gave the poor their table scraps, much less held conversations with them. *That* may have gone down the drain years ago, Helen thought, but it was certainly still true in high school. Cheerleader types simply didn't associate with frizzy-haired new girls who looked two years too young, locked themselves out of their lockers, and drew political cartoons.

Mercifully Miss Podell forgot about her sixty seconds of silence almost the moment she announced it. The bell rang, and the class surged out toward the early buses.

Helen was sure, as she wended her way up to the history room, that the last catastrophe of the day lay waiting for her with Mr. Brzostoski. He was probably Polish, she decided. Most likely the Russians had tortured his family to death and he had escaped to America, where everything was beautiful and wonderful. He probably didn't like criticism of anything modern or American and would hate her for her drawing. He would probably think she was a Communist.

Helen stood in the history room doorway, patiently watching him eat another banana while he marked his attendance sheets. Suddenly he noticed her and smiled.

"Your six pages were excellent!" he said. "Where did you learn so much history?"

"From my father," Helen answered, smiling too and looking at his banana hungrily.

"Hungry?"

"Oh, *am* I! I locked all my stuff in my locker this morning by mistake. My lunch too."

Mr. Bro handed her a banana. "Eat!" he said, and to it he added a Hershey bar. Helen was pleased to see that despite all the bananas he was not a health-food freak. He held her cartoon up. "This," he said, "is the best drawing to pass my desk in years."

The pleasure that burst like a tiny firework inside Helen must have shown in her face, and Mr. Bro was evidently waiting for it. He smiled even more broadly. "Now we have work to do," he announced.

Helen had been sure that pleasure itself had ceased to exist the moment she'd left St. Theresa's and come to New Bedford Regional. "Work?" she asked.

"You know the *Whaler* downstairs? The school paper?"

"I think so. Down in the basement of the other building?"

"That's it. Now listen. The editor of the *Whaler,* Jerry Rosen, is a big shot. He wants only one thing in his life."

"What's that?" asked Helen.

"He wants to go to Yale. But he needs a scholarship.

He wants to win the ten thousand dollar grant that the City of New Bedford gives out every June. He knows he'll win it hands down if he gets the prize for journalism that the state awards every year to the best high school newspaper. Jerry is a very good editor, don't get me wrong, but he has a soft spot."

Mr. Bro coughed, twisted his ring, and looked Helen square in the eyes. "I usually don't talk to students this way," he said, "especially brand-new ones, but . . . somehow it's hard to think of you as brand new." He grinned. Then he began writing a note on a yellow legal pad.

Helen felt also that Mr. Bro wasn't brand new like her other teachers. She listened.

"I want to help Jerry," Mr. Bro went on. "He isn't a wealthy boy. He's a good editor and a fine student, and he deserves to go to Yale. His soft spot, unfortunately, is his girl friend, Beverly Boone." He kept writing, seeming to choose his words carefully. "Beverly's going to be the death of Jerry's state journalism award. She does these awful, sappy editorial cartoons for the *Whaler* every week. Last year I was faculty advisor to the *Whaler,* and Jerry was managing editor. I couldn't get him to stop printing these disgusting little caterpillar drawings she turns out. Now the time has come to get Jerry to print an editorial cartoon with some guts to it."

Helen nodded. "But," she said, "if you couldn't get him to change his mind last year when you were advisor, how can you get him to do it this year when you're not?"

Mr. Bro grinned again, this time mischievously. "Beverly's gone into business," he said smoothly. "Now she cuts her little smily-faced caterpillars out of copper, enamels them in livid colors, bakes them in the school kiln, and sells them at drugstores. She makes a pretty penny at it using school materials! I haven't told the principal, but if I do, he'll stop her. She's making a private profit off the school. She says it's an art project, but it's a business. If I stop Beverly using the school kiln, she'll hit the roof. Jerry Rosen will do anything for Beverly. He's in love. If I tell him to run your cartoon instead of Beverly's caterpillars or else, he will. Believe me. It will help the *Whaler*. It will help Jerry win his state journalism award and get his scholarship. I'm doing him a favor. He must put some ideas and controversy into that paper, or he'll fail. If I have to give him a little nudge in the right direction, he'll do it, and since he won't listen to reason, he'll listen to Beverly." Mr. Bro clipped his note on top of Helen's drawing. "Another thing," he said softly. He began straightening the papers on his desk. "You see, what you have in that drawing is an idea. It's funny, and you are a very talented artist, but the important thing is, it's full of heart and caring. It's got thinking behind it. The caterpillars . . . I can't tell you what a waste I think it is that such claptrap is printed, even in a school newspaper. Beverly has the heart of a Hostess Twinkie. Now . . . go down to the *Whaler* office. Give Jerry this cartoon and this note, and you'll be in like Flynn!"

"Thank you, Mr. Brzostoski," said Helen a little breathlessly.

"Bro," said Mr. Brzostoski. "Bro is much easier."

She turned around once more in the doorway, but he

was already busily locking up his drawers. Then her feet were running down the empty hall toward the *Whaler* office. There, she knew, either acceptance as warm as a tropical sea or a still greater disaster to end this day of wretchedness awaited her.

TWO

"You must have come about the booster tags!" chirped an optimistic voice when Helen stepped into the *Whaler* office. "I'm Penny Parker, assistant business manager," the girl went on without waiting for a reply. She shook a full head of copper curls as merrily as she spoke. "It's just super of you to come and help us. How many tags do you think you can sell this week? Fifty? A hundred?"

"I . . . um, what exactly are they?" asked Helen.

"My goodness!" said Penny. She hauled a carton to where Helen was standing and ripped the tape and flaps off the top of it. Then she plunged her hand into a mass of little white cardboard triangles, each with a string attached and each with a picture of a football player and the message "BEAT FALL RIVER!" in red ink. "Aren't they great?" asked Penny. "What you do is, you sell them to all your friends, and they get everyone else to sign 'em. You hang 'em on your notebook ring or on your pocketbook. You sell 'em for fifty cents apiece and bring us the money at the end of the week. You should do real well this week 'cause Fall River's our big rival!"

"I really came," said Helen, "with a note for Jerry—the editor?" She edged the note and drawing, upside down, into Penny's view. Penny was counting out tags. She stopped and blinked at Helen.

"You mean you won't help us out?" asked Penny. "Gee, when you're a freshman, it's a great way to meet all the kids!"

Helen was terrified of annoying this pert and important girl, but she could not imagine having fifty friends to sell tags to, and worst of all she knew she would never have the heart to sell anything with such a bad drawing on it. "Of course I'll help!" she said, only hoping Penny would begin to smile again. Penny giggled. "I'll take that right in to Jerry," she said. "You just stay here and count out your tags. Be right back!"

Around Helen typewriters clattered. A telephone rang again and again. People, all older than she, laughed and catcalled at one another. She turned a booster tag over in her hand. She warned herself not to say anything. Not to volunteer to do the football player drawing over and ask to have them reprinted. *Listen, Helen,* she told herself sharply, *don't make any mistakes. If they print this cartoon of yours, maybe they'll print another and then another, and then you'll never have to envy the cheerleaders again. You'll never have to worry about being asked to join things because you will already be a part of something on your own. Don't mess it up!* she added. *Keep your big mouth shut!*

"Well, he wants to see you," said Penny with a shrug. She startled Helen, who dropped several tags on the floor.

The editor's office was in a metal cubicle the color of a Band-Aid. Three people stared at her as if she had just played a cruel joke on them. She felt like an ant.

She guessed that Jerry Rosen was the one in the middle chair, behind the enormous oak desk. The desk was much more impressive than any of the teachers' metal ones upstairs. Jerry dressed like a movie-version editor. He actually wore a vest. It was unbuttoned. His sleeves were rolled up just so at the elbows, and his tie was loosened slightly at his unbuttoned collar. "Sit down, sit down," he said, indicating a folding chair. Helen guessed the legs had been sawn off an inch or two because her head just came up to the level of the desk when she sat in it. A pallid, bland-looking young man sat on Jerry's left, and a dreamy blond girl who was trying to conceal a piece of gum behind a back tooth lounged at his right. Helen could not keep her eyes off Jerry's jittery hands or his dark, wavy hair.

"Well, well, well," Jerry began. He swiveled around in his executive chair and plopped his Top-siders on the desk. "Seems as if you have some drawing potential, Helen."

"Thank you," said Helen. She knew she was dead in the water. "Potential" was not much of a compliment after what Mr. Bro had said.

"You certainly seem to have some strong ideas about

the President of the United States and the governor of Massachusetts, not to mention nuclear power plants."

"Well, yes," Helen said miserably.

"Just explain this to me," said Jerry, squinting at the drawing as if he needed glasses. "The President? The governor? It says here 'drinking heavy water and eating yellow cake'? Is that it?"

"Heavy water," Helen said, trying to keep her voice from cracking, "is contaminated cooling water used in nuclear power plants. Yellow cake is the stuff that spills out of the trucks that carry the waste. If one of the waste-carrying trucks got in an accident and spilled the yellow cake all over the highway, thousands, millions of people could get killed. They come right through New Bedford, those trucks, on their way from the Pilgrim Nuclear Plant in Plymouth. They should be stopped!"

The young man at Jerry's side clucked his tongue but did not look up from a sheaf of papers.

"First of all," said Jerry, "a high school newspaper simply doesn't run cartoons showing the President and the governor in very unflattering poses. Secondly, what you say is nonsense. The trucks are perfectly safe."

"They're not," said Helen. "What would happen if that Punk Rock Thrower, the one who's been throwing rocks at cars . . . supposing he hit a nuclear-waste truck. It could wipe out half of New England!"

"Barry?" said Jerry. He looked over to his left. "Barry, what would Mr. Perry say if he saw a cartoon like this in the *Whaler*?" Jerry turned to Helen for a second and added, "Barry works part time for Perry and Crowe downtown."

"Oh," answered Barry, shaking his head, "Mr. Perry'd be very upset by a cartoon like that. Why, he'd probably take all his advertising out of the *Whaler*."

"I think every businessman in New Bedford would do the same, don't you, Barry?" Jerry asked.

"The businessmen support the Pilgrim plant," said Barry. "They certainly wouldn't like a lot of left-wing controversy in a school newspaper with their advertisements. They might lose money. They'd all take their ads out of the *Whaler,* and then the *Whaler* would go broke. I'm sure you'd have a lot of trouble if you ran that cartoon."

"You see, Helen," said Jerry, smiling, "we can't afford to lose our advertising money. We'd be out of business in a week. You don't want to ruin the *Whaler,* do you, Helen?"

"Well, of course I don't," said Helen, "but—"

"And you wouldn't want the *Whaler* to lose out on a chance of winning the state journalism prize because of your cartoon, would you, Helen?"

"Oh, no," said Helen, "but—"

"The choice is up to you," said Jerry. "If you tell us just to forget the cartoon, we'll give it back to you, and everything will be okay."

"Choice? Up to me?" Helen asked.

"I realize you're kind of disappointed," Jerry added so unctuously Helen's toes curled. "Tell you what I'll do. If freshmen want to work for the *Whaler,* they have to sell booster tags. Sophomores get to carry equipment and collect ad money from the local merchants. Only when you get to be a junior do you get to join the *Whaler* staff for real. Now, I think a girl with your brains and potential would be bored selling booster tags or collecting ad money. How would you like to come right on the *Whaler* staff? Right now! Beverly here is the staff artist. Maybe she'll let you help her with a little of the paste-up. How about it, Bev?"

"Sure," said Beverly languidly. Beverly's blond hair was, if anything, more glowing and perfect than the girl's in the pink frosted sweater. Helen coughed. She wondered what paste-up was.

Jerry opened his drawer. He took out a little red and white button with the school crest and the words *Whaler Press Pass* on it and flipped it to the edge of the desk, just within Helen's reach. "This will be your press pass," he said. "Gets you into all football and basketball games free. You get to miss one class a day, study hall or gym, as a staff member. This very week, Helen, if you say yes, your own paste-up will appear printed in the *Whaler*'s first issue."

Helen was stunned. She did not answer. Jerry apparently took this for hesitation. "Tell you what else I'll do," he said. "Barry here has brought in the ad for Perry and Crowe's fall sale. How would you like to do the drawing for the Perry and Crowe ad and see it printed right there in the *Whaler*?"

Barry gave Jerry a sour look. "Bev's supposed to do it, Jerry," he said. "I don't see why this freshman—"

"Let's give her a chance, Barry. Okay?" said Jerry. "What do you say, Helen? Are you going to make us lose out on the state award and give up all our advertising, or do you want to start off your high school career as the *Whaler*'s staff art assistant?"

Helen's hand closed over the little red and white button. Everyone in the room relaxed. Beverly started chewing her gum again, lazily. Helen knew that none of them would care if a nuclear truck rolled over and blew up so long as it didn't bother them. "Show her what you want, Barry," said Jerry, folding Helen's drawing into a square the size of a postage stamp.

Barry took a box gently from between his knees and placed it on the desk. "I'm Barry de Wolf," he said, and Helen felt she ought to salute. "Don't break this. It's a fifty-dollar music box." Helen watched as he removed the tissue from around a Hummel figurine. This one was a statuette of a little German boy in lederhosen. He was carrying a staff, and skipping behind him was either a lamb or a goat. Helen couldn't tell. Hummel figurines were among her Aunt Stella's favorite collectibles. She owned four. Helen hated them. She hated their pink cheeks, cupid bow smiles, and the frantic little tunes they played. "Oh, he's just beautiful," she said as Barry unwrapped him.

"Mr. Perry," said Barry, "wants him drawn just the way he is, except leave out the goat and the staff and make his arm bend up as if he's saying 'Come on in!' Do you think you can do that? Do you think you can make him really cute? Mr. Perry wants him really cute."

"Oh, I think so," said Helen. She hoped this would lead to better things.

With shaking hands Helen placed the figurine in its

tissue and its box and then slipped it into her pocketbook.

"You're not going to swing that pocketbook around, are you?" Barry asked.

"Oh, no," said Helen. "I was just . . ." She fumbled and took the box out again. She held it with both hands.

"Take the stairway on the right," said Jerry. "Go down to the pressroom. Pinky Levy is printing hall passes down there. Ask him to show you how to do paste-up. If you need help, call on Bev."

Beverly waved three fingers. She did not look helpful.

Helen turned to go. "Do you suppose," she asked shyly, telling herself sternly to shut up, "if I gave you some drawings of football players and you liked them, maybe we could print up a new set of booster tags?"

A silence answered this. Beverly raised an eyebrow. Jerry finally said, "Sure. Sure." Barry watched the box in Helen's hands as if it were about to explode of its own accord.

Helen recognized the cowlick on the back of Pinky's head immediately.

"Get your locker open yet?" he asked when he turned around. Pinky was on his knees tinkering with an old printing press in the lowest basement room of the building. There were no windows. A flickering fluorescent light hung above a grimy drawing board.

"No," said Helen. She hoped that it wouldn't be "her" drawing board.

"When I'm finished here, I'll open it for you," said Pinky. "Couldn't do it this morning. Too many people around for me to hear the works in the lock."

Helen waited a decent interval. The press began to creak and shudder into action. Huge sheets of pink paper floated to the floor one after another. "Those'll get dirty," said Helen. "Let me pick them up."

Pinky squeegeed three gobs of printer's ink onto one of the rollers. "Don't go near the press," he said. "You'll get hurt."

"I won't get hurt," said Helen.

"Girls don't know anything about the power of machinery," said Pinky. "My sister nearly lost her hand in the toaster because she doesn't understand how it works. Sit over there, why don't you? How come you came down here?"

"I'm on the *Whaler* staff," said Helen proudly. "Jerry said you'd be able to show me how to do paste-up?"

Pinky laughed. "So they finally found someone sucker enough to do Beverly's dirty work!" he said.

"But it's an honor!" Helen protested. "I don't have to sell tags or collect ad money. My work gets printed!"

"The thrill will wear off after five minutes," said Pinky.

Helen wished she could leave this awful room and this bossy boy. She did not want to go home without her books, however, and there was a chance he might open her locker, so she sat down with a stack of old *Whaler*s and waited.

The first thing she looked for was Beverly's caterpillar cartoons. Helen could see Mr. Bro's point. One caterpillar was called Moonbeam. He said things like "Gee, there must be more to life than drinking nectar. I bet there's a butterfly inside each and every one of us."

One issue contained a story that had won a prize, a

gold medal, in fact, for the story of the year. Barry de Wolf had written it, and it was entitled "Non-migratory Birds of New Bedford, an In-depth Study." Helen's eyes closed. She yawned. Suddenly she said, "Oh, dear . . . there's a spelling mistake on the hall passes you're printing."

"What?" asked Pinky. He stopped the press. It came to a slow, dying halt, clanking all the while.

"Right here," said Helen. "The word *message* is spelled m-a-s-s-a-g-e. That's a back rub, a massage."

Pinky swore under his breath. "It *isn't* wrong," he said.

"It is," said Helen.

Pinky swore again. "You better be right about this," he said. "This means I'll have to send out for a new plate, and Jerry'll kill me because of the expense."

"I'm sorry," said Helen. "I didn't mean to make trouble for you."

"Well, you have."

"But it isn't my fault. It isn't your fault either. You just printed it."

"It *is* my fault," said Pinky. "I did the paste-up on it, and I should have caught it. Beverly was too lazy, bless her snaky little heart. Boy, I bet Bev's laughing in her beer 'cause she shoved the paste-up job off on some dumb freshman!"

Helen's happiness had faded altogether by this time. Meekly she followed Pinky up the stairs toward her locker. Pinky marched on ahead like a soldier, muttering about how much it would cost to remake the plate and about how much time and paper was involved in reprinting the hall passes.

"Okay," he said when they reached the door of Miss Podell's classroom. "Which one is it?"

All the lockers looked alike in the vast, empty hallway. Helen took a deep breath and pointed. "This one," she said.

Pinky bent down and put his ear to the lock. He twirled the dial. It opened.

"Oh, thank you," said Helen. She looked into the locker. It contained only a pair of boy's gym shorts. "I think it's the locker next to this one," she said, squeezing her eyes shut.

Pinky stooped again. His face was scarlet with anger. "Boy," he said, "there are certain types of people in this world. Know-it-all types. Always pointing the finger at somebody else. Always finding piddling little mistakes. But when it comes to their own mistakes, watch out! Help me, help me! It's not *my* fault. Now, is this the right locker, or do you want me to open all of them?"

With relief Helen removed her own books, lunch, and binder.

"Know-it-all types can't think their way out of a paper bag," said Pinky.

Unfortunately it appeared that Pinky was headed for the same bus as Helen. They walked in silence on opposite sides of the hall. They sat in silence on the nearly empty bus, he in the front seat and she way in the back. In her imagination Helen began dreaming up what she wanted to say to Pinky. *There are people in this world,* she decided she would say, *who blame everything on everyone else.* That didn't sound nearly dramatic enough. *Men have been responsible for all the wars in history,* she began again. The bus lurched to a stop. Pinky swung himself out the door. *Whereas if women were in charge of things, there would be no—* Suddenly Helen realized this was her stop too. She couldn't very well stay on the bus— Aunt Stella would be beside herself with worry right now. She was probably reporting Helen to the police as a missing person this very minute. Helen got off, books stacked unevenly in her sweating arms and the Hummel figurine bumping heavily against her side in her pocketbook. She walked ten paces behind Pinky. Aunt Stella was going to call the Board of Ed to change Helen's bus route, as she didn't like Helen's being dropped off on a highway ten minutes away from home. Helen hoped Aunt Stella would succeed. She didn't look forward to walking home with Pinky every day.

She filled her lungs with air. "You male chauvinist pig!" she yelled. "You probably can't even spell your own name!" But at that exact moment a truck passed them, scattering gravel onto the shoulder of the road. Its noise drowned out her words but not a sudden crash of splintering glass.

The truck vanished down the highway, but a car that had been just behind it skidded and spun in a complete circle fifty feet ahead of them. There was a scream that went on and on. Helen and Pinky dropped their books and ran toward the car. A little girl of about four was wailing piteously.

Time suddenly became an elastic substance. Helen found her eyes riveted to the broken windshield glass. It had shattered into bits like dollhouse-size ice cubes all over the car and roadway. She brushed some of it off the little girl's dress. She saw the reddish iron rock on the front seat. It looked like the piece of iron ore in the Riches of Our Earth display in the Museum of Science.

Was it an hour that she was hypnotized by the winking glass and the rock or just a few seconds? Pinky was examining the woman in the driver's seat. Helen held the little girl and tried to comfort her. Her breath came in short gasps, the way she imagined it would on top of a high mountain, and yet she felt too that everything was happening underwater. She noticed herself sinking to her knees while a voice both inside her head and miles away outside yelled, "What kind of person are you? Get ahold of yourself, you silly jerk, and help these people!" She was too dizzy to obey until she realized it was Pinky's voice. He was shaking her shoulder and shouting in her ear.

"Damn it!" he said. "Don't be such a stupid gutless *girl*!"

The car seat came into focus again. The woman was draped across it. Pure, healthy anger washed over Helen. She placed the little girl in the back seat, making sure there was no glass there. The blood from the woman's wound was turning black against the upholstery, soaking in.

Pinky tore his shirt into strips. "Help me," he yelled, "you airhead!"

There were two shopping bags of groceries that had spilled onto the pavement. Helen took a roll of paper towels, ripped off a bunch, dipped them in a handy container of milk, and cleaned the woman's face and some arm wounds. The little girl in the back seat kept trying to tumble over to her mother. Her hair was matted, her face full of tears and snot, and she continued to scream hysterically. Helen held the child off with one hand and tucked Pinky's shirt bandages snug and tight with the other hand.

"That's practically a tourniquet. I'm going to loosen it," said Pinky.

"Don't touch it," said Helen. "You want her to bleed to death?"

"You want her to lose an arm?" asked Pinky.

"It's an artery!" Helen insisted. "It's pumping. Don't make it looser. You have to stop arterial bleeding with a tight bandage."

"Artery, my eye!" said Pinky. "You cut off the blood supply, she'll lose an arm. It's a vein. It's superficial."

"I took first aid with Sister de Angelis, who spent five years in Africa!" said Helen. "And she told us—"

"Yeah?" Pinky broke in. "I had four years of first aid in the Boy Scouts of America, and I know what I'm talking about."

In a quieter moment Helen would have admitted that her knowledge of first aid was sketchy to say the least. All she could really recall was Sister de Angelis's treatment for fire-ant bites. "The bleeding's stopped, Pinky. Leave the bandage alone!" she said between gritted teeth. "You touch that bandage, and the woman will die."

"I'm not going to die," whispered the woman. Pinky and Helen both stared at the yellow-white face under the bloody dark hair. The woman was struggling to sit up. Pinky strode into the middle of the highway. He scanned it, looking up and down for a car, but the highway was as empty as a desert. *"Somebody come!"* he yelled in desperation after a few minutes.

Helen spotted the house, partially hidden by trees úp on the side of the hill. She guessed it was occupied, as for a moment she saw someone standing outside it. No cars came. "Help!" Helen yelled up to the house. "Call the police! Get an ambulance!"

"Somebody there?" asked Pinky.

"Up the hill," said Helen, pointing to the house. "They just went in to call. Help is on the way," she assured the woman. "Everything's going to be all right."

"We've got to get out of here!" Pinky yelled. "The gas tank might blow up any minute. I can smell it."

The woman could walk, a little unsteadily. Pinky helped her, letting her lean on him. Helen carried the child up the hill.

"You should never have used milk to clean those wounds," said Pinky. "Milk's full of bacteria."

Fear rippled through Helen's being. Her hands began to shake and her mouth dried up. Bacteria! What had Sister de Angelis said about bacteria? Africa was full of hundreds of kinds. Sister de Angelis had never made a move in those five years without a canteen of purified drinking water, because of bacteria, and another full of alcohol, for bacteria also. Sister had passed around the classroom an old tin of vile-smelling antibacterial ointment good for fire-ant bites. Helen wished Pinky would step in a nest of fire ants right that minute.

The little girl sobbed with a jagged regularity that would not wind down.

Pinky tried the front door of the house. It was locked. He rapped sharply on it, yelling for someone to come. When no one did, he leaned the woman up against Helen, like a broom, and jimmied open a window. "Thought you said someone was here," he snorted angrily.

The woman slid down and sat on the front steps of the house. Helen still held the fighting, tearful child. "But there was someone here," she said to no one in particular. "There *was*." The little girl kicked against her hip. "Nice little girl," said Helen. Helen did not like children very much. "Here," she continued. "Nice apple! See the nice apple?" She picked the least wormy crab apple she could reach from the low-hanging branch of an apple tree. It was the tree where she was sure she'd seen the person standing. The child grabbed the apple and took a bite. Immediately she spat it out and began to howl again. A rake and a roll of chicken wire leaned against the trunk of the tree. *I guess that was what I saw,* Helen said to herself sadly. *And it looked like a person. Just like a mirage in the desert.*

The little girl threw the sour apple angrily to the ground. Two feet away from it was another apple. It too had a bite taken out of it, freshly, because the edges were not yet brown.

Pinky opened the front door of the house from the inside. He bent and lifted the woman to her feet. Gently he led her inside to a sofa. The little girl's screams echoed through the quiet house like a squash ball madly bouncing off the walls of an indoor court, gaining momentum. Then they stopped, as if an alarm had been turned off, when Helen laid her gently next to her mother. The woman focused on the child's face, seemed satisfied, and with her free hand began searching through her child's hair.

"The cops are coming," said Pinky. "I just talked to them. Take 'em ten minutes to get a squad car out here. They said to give the lady some brandy if I can find any."

Helen stroked the woman's injured arm distractedly and assured her that her groceries didn't matter a bit. She gazed out the window beside her. The distant wild scrub oak became scrub pine and then real woods far beyond on the hillside. In the middle distance a field of rye grass and goldenrod undulated tranquilly, blithely denying the violence of the last few minutes. Helen was on the point of asking Pinky whether they'd get into trouble for breaking and entering a house when she saw someone moving between two faraway trees.

Pinky came back from the kitchen with a Dixie cup of strong-smelling liquor.

Helen jumped to her feet. "There's somebody out there going up the hill into the woods!" she said and ran out the door.

Pinky could only yell after her, "Wait a minute! Maybe it's the guy who threw the rock at the car!"

The running was easy. She jumped over hummocks of grass and low ditches like a rabbit. She reached the spot where she'd seen the person and decided she would have a better chance of catching up to him if she headed straight for where she guessed he was going rather than trying to follow the path, so she cut around the scrub pines directly into the deeper woods. It occurred to her then that he had not been running at all but was walking very deliberately.

Raggedy branches were scattered all over the ground

around her. Every one of her footfalls sounded to Helen like a starting pistol. Rough bark and vines caught at her hair, and the trees themselves seemed to have come alive with noise.

Her body heaved with the effort of the uphill running. Stinging scratches from the rough bark and nettle bushes burned her arms and legs and face. A particularly nasty hooked branch snarled her hair, and she stopped to free it. Then she heard someone coming up the hill just behind her.

She tried to calm her panic and think sensibly. *I can run off to the side,* she thought suddenly. *But if I have a chance to see him . . .*

Helen found an overturned stump with a hundred dead roots in the air, like so many desperately reaching claws. She lay down beneath it and dug herself into the soft humus and pine needles. She listened as he came closer, walking up the grassy deer run just a few feet away. *I wish I'd run away,* she thought. It was too late now to go anywhere. She pressed her mother's picture, which hung in a silver locket around her throat, with a trembling hand. *Mother, Mother. Please be with me. God help me,* she prayed. *Don't let him find me. I only did this because that stupid Pinky Levy called me a gutless girl.* She dug herself deeper into the earth beneath the stump. The footsteps were seconds away. Far down on the highway the sirens of the police car began to wail followed by the howling Klaxon of an ambulance At that moment he passed the stump where she lay hidden. He was much too close to her, just inches away, for her to see anything of him. The cuff of a pair of chinos, a white sweat sock with a

burr stuck on it, an old white Nike sneaker with the *e* in
Nike worn off. There was a spring to his step. When he'd
gone a dozen strides farther up the hill, she raised her
head and for a tick of a second saw only the back of
someone so obscured by the rippling leaves of the ash
trees, she knew she would never be able to describe him to
anyone. She kept her eyes on the last bit of his white
T-shirt, and then he seemed to vanish into a high rock
covered with poison ivy and nettles up ahead.

Helen backed out of her hiding place as soundlessly
and slickly as a snake uncoiling. She ran faster down the
hill than she had ever known she had the power to do.

She did not stop until she'd reached the center of the
field of rye grass, where she sat down heavily. Her throat
had closed, and she thought she'd never be able to breathe
again. *He didn't see me,* she said to herself over and over.
He didn't see me. Or did he? Had he hidden himself and
watched, smiling, from behind the leaves of a tree?

And why would he be smiling? The answer to this
would not come, but she was quite sure of it all the same.
A stitch ached excruciatingly in her side. She held it, unable to get up again until it went away. She had picked up
more scratches and bruises in her tumbling, headlong race
down the hill. Finally Helen got to her feet and tried to
make the best of her appearance. She tried to picture what
little she'd seen of him. There was nothing to picture.
Everything about him was as ordinary as the hundreds of
people who had sat next to her on park benches or in
buses and whom she'd never noticed or remembered. *He
couldn't have seen me,* she told herself again.

Puzzled, Helen realized that since she'd gotten up and

begun walking back to the house, she'd been humming. She stopped herself. Helen was not the kind of person who went around humming.

Suddenly she knew why. She was humming without thinking because the man in the woods had been whistling. Whistling quite happily, and that was why she had thought that if he'd seen her, he'd be smiling.

She hummed the melody once over, but the name of it and the words would not come. She looked back up the hill. He was somewhere there in the profound depths of the woods, but all she could say about him was that he whistled, and he whistled perfectly, liltingly, sweetly, with dulcet double notes, like a flute or a nightingale with an astonishingly haunting call.

THREE

"Name please?" asked the police officer after he'd taken in Helen's appearance.

"Helen Curragh, Five Twenty-five Prospect Avenue," said Helen. She'd caught sight of herself in a mirror on the way into the house. Her skirt was torn at the hem, her face crisscrossed with ugly scratches, and her hair a wild mass of curls, dotted with leaves. Her clothes were entirely covered with smears of earth.

"Well, Helen, you've certainly done a job on yourself," said the policeman with a broad grin.

"I saw him!" said Helen. "I saw the Punk Rock Thrower. I went up in the woods after him, and I saw him!"

"Hold your horses," said the policeman. He inched a

worn leather notebook out from one of his fat pockets, licked his thumb, opened it, and sat down on the sofa. "Okay, honey. Who'd you see?"

"The rock thrower," Helen began.

"Did you see him throw the rock at the car?" asked the policeman.

"Well, not actually, but—"

"You didn't see him throw the rock?"

"No, but he was watching, from in front of this house, while we were yelling for help down at the road. I thought he lived in this house. I thought he went in to call for help. But the house was empty when we got here. He must have run away."

"So you followed him?"

"No. Not just then. We had to get the lady and the little girl up the hill to the house. Pinky was afraid of the gas tank catching fire, so we sort of carried them up here. . . ."

"And how did you get into the house?" asked the policeman.

"A window was open," said Pinky quickly. Pinky was squirming in a hard-backed chair, quite impatiently.

At least the policeman hadn't called him *"honey,"* Helen thought.

The policeman went on in a monotone. "So you didn't actually see this person run away?"

"No, sir. I saw him later through the window. Then I chased after him."

"And he ran."

"No, he walked."

"Walked? How do you know it was the same person?"

"I . . . It had to be."

"I see. Describe him."

"I didn't see him."

"I thought you said you saw him."

"Well, I did, but . . ."

"How do you know it wasn't a woman?"

"Because . . . because it wasn't. I hid under a stump. I could just see his jogging shoes. Nikes. But he was whistling. It wasn't a woman's whistling—"

"*Whistling!*" The policeman snapped shut his report book. "Honey, you saw a jogger," he said.

"Now wait just a cotton pickin' minute," Pinky interjected. "This girl did the number-one bravest thing I ever saw anybody do, and you won't let her get a word in edgewise."

The policeman stood and sighed good-naturedly. "Keep your pants on, son," he said. "Your girl friend was, first of all, very foolish to follow *anybody* up through the woods. You are good, helpful kids, but that was stupid." He let this sink in while Pinky fidgeted and Helen tried to keep from shouting at him in frustration. "Now, second of all, she didn't see any rock thrown. She doesn't know if it was a man, woman, or child in the woods. It was probably a jogger—"

"He wasn't jogging," interrupted Helen.

"Who knows?" said the policeman. "There's even an old Indian who lives up in the woods somewhere."

"He wasn't old," Helen insisted.

"If it was the guy who threw the rock," the policeman drawled on, as if she'd said nothing, "he'd have run away. Look, there's even some company, a contractor, been talking about building a condominium up here for ten years. She might have seen a land surveyor. We get a hundred witnesses to every dog bite in this business."

"I heard the police sirens way up in the woods," said Helen, "and the ambulance when it came for the woman and the little girl. I could tell. The sound is different. He had to have heard them too. He knew you were too far away to catch him. If it wasn't the rock thrower, why didn't he even turn around?"

"Believe me, honey," said the policeman, "the guy who threw the rock through the windshield would have run like a deer. *Especially* if he heard the sirens. He's probably in the next county by now."

Helen did not bother to mention the apple.

Another policeman stuck his head in the door. "Ready to go," he said.

"We'll send you both good citizenship awards," said the first policeman kindly, "and, honey, don't go chasing guys through the woods anymore. You might get more than your pretty dress messed up next time."

Pinky and Helen trudged down the hill. They both spoke at once. "Thanks for sticking up for me," said Helen. "Want a ride home?" asked Pinky. They laughed.

"A ride?" asked Helen.

Pinky glanced around, as if the bushes contained microphones. "I keep a trail bike not far from here," he said in a low voice. "There's room for two on it."

Helen wanted to ask if it was illegal, but she decided it was and didn't ask.

They walked down the hill to the highway and collected their books and Helen's pocketbook, which the policemen had thoughtfully heaped against a guardrail.

Helen tried to remember the tune the man had been whistling. She'd forgotten it cleanly.

Pinky led Helen away from the road, down into a dried-up ditch. Beyond that, under a tangle of wild grapevines, was a decrepit shed, its roof caved in and most of the walls destroyed by a long-ago fire. Just inside was a sheet of burned plywood; out from under it Pinky pulled a very old motorcycle. "It isn't really a trail bike," he said. "But I thought you might get scared if I said motorcycle."

"It isn't really a motorcycle either," said Helen, looking at it curiously.

"Oh, but it is," Pinky answered proudly. "World War Two German Army bike. My dad picked it up when he was young in an Army surplus store. I got it fixed so it runs like a champ. Got a super muffler on it too. Doesn't make any more noise than a refrigerator."

Helen, wondering what Aunt Stella would think if she could see her now, sat down on the back of the bike, locked her arms and hands around Pinky's middle, and held on to him as if she were about to take a rocket to the moon.

"Not so tight!" Pinky objected. "It only goes ten miles an hour! I can't breathe with you hanging on like that!"

Helen relaxed. Pinky was right. The bike made almost no noise at all. He headed it onto a trail that ran in a different direction from the one she'd followed to the deep woods. The only sound was the flapping of their books in the two saddlebags against the exhaust pipes.

Pinky cleared his throat. "Sorry for being such a grouch before," he said.

"That's all right," said Helen. "It's got to be a royal

pain in the neck to have some freshman come up to you after a hard day's work and tell you you made a spelling mistake."

"I'm a freshman too," he said after a minute.

"I thought . . . you were older," said Helen. "The *Whaler* people know you . . ."

"Left back a year," Pinky answered.

"Oh, I'm sorry," said Helen, as if she'd stumbled on a death in the family.

"Going to quit school when I'm sixteen next year," Pinky went on. "I hate school. I hate books. I'm not cut out for a desk job, so I'm going to jump a freighter and then join the Navy as soon as I'm old enough. Meantime I like printing for the *Whaler*. My uncle's a printer. It gets in your blood."

"Well," said Helen, "if you want help with homework, give me a call. It must be awful to hate books and school and have to take tests on the Revolutionary War and *Silas Marner*."

"We have a test Monday," said Pinky. "History."

"Come over and study Sunday," said Helen.

"Lemme know when I can return the favor," Pinky answered stiffly.

Helen calculated. "Saturday," she said.

"Saturday?"

"I want to do some drawings of football players to make decent-looking booster tags. I'm sort of embarrassed to go to the game alone," she explained wistfully, "and—"

"It's a deal," said Pinky. "Gee, you're a funny girl."

"Why?"

"Just because."

For several minutes they rode in silence. Then Helen asked quietly, "Did you believe me? About the man in the woods? I mean about it being strange that he didn't help and he was just walking away whistling?"

"Yup," said Pinky shortly. "But if the cops don't believe you, forget it. Cops!" he said. "Cops wouldn't believe a kid if you told them the sun was out."

"We better get off here," Helen said. "My Aunt Stella'd have a fit if she saw me on a motorbike."

Pinky stopped and parked the motorcycle against a tree. The first houses along Prospect Avenue were a minute away. "Who's Aunt Stella?" he asked.

"My dad's sister. She lives with us. My mom died years ago. Pinky . . ." She frowned. The song was coming back now. At first she could hum only a few notes. Then the tune unfolded like a well rehearsed chant. "It's a hiking song, Pinky. We used to sing it at camp. Something about wandering through the mountains with a knapsack." Helen sang several lines of it ending with the chorus ". . . *Valderi, valdera.* . . . Pinky, what's the name of that song?"

"I don't know," said Pinky. "It's just one of those songs. Kind of like 'Oh, What a Beautiful Morning.' "

"Well, that's what the man was whistling. Pinky, it makes no sense. He had to have thrown the rock. Of *course* he walked away whistling. He's a nut. He didn't know I was after him, and he knew he'd get away from the cops easily. They didn't show up for ten minutes. He was already a mile away up in the woods when the sirens started."

Pinky clucked his tongue. "Won't do any good to think about it," he said. "Even if the cops did catch him, they'd probably put him away for two months in a nuthouse. Good behavior and he'd be out in thirty days. For what he did they ought to give him a buzz in the chair."

"Thank *God*!" said Aunt Stella. Her hand rested against her heart as she led Pinky and Helen into the house and sat herself down on a button-plush settee. "I just notified the police that you were missing," she said, adjusting her silk flower-print dress over her motherly, comfortable bulk. "Who is this, Helen?"

"This is Pinky Levy, Aunt Stella. He—"

"Well, I think it's time he went home to his mother," said Aunt Stella. "The policeman on the telephone told me all about what you've been up to. You look a fright, Helen. What on earth were you doing running up into the woods after a lunatic?" Aunt Stella looked over at Pinky, who seemed rooted to the rug. "I repeat, young man, I believe you'll be wanted at home."

"Yes, ma'am," said Pinky. "Pleasure to meet you."

"Good-bye," said Aunt Stella.

Pinky backed out the door.

"Now, tell me what this is all about, young lady! You could have been killed. Molested! Wait till I tell your father!"

Helen went into the kitchen and made two cups of tea. While the water boiled, she let Aunt Stella boil, and when Aunt Stella could think of nothing more to say and had finished her tea, Helen told her about the little girl crying and the injured mother. "I tried to be a good citizen, Aunt Stella," she said.

"I suppose," Aunt Stella said, slightly mollified.

"And wait till I tell you about my terrific new job on the school paper. They gave me a junior's job, Aunt Stella!" Helen went on about the press badge and the paste-up and the ad for Perry and Crowe.

Aunt Stella was duly impressed and much happier when Helen had assured her that no freshman had ever had such a job in the history of the school.

"Now I think it's time for a bath," said Aunt Stella. "You look like Attila the Hun."

Helen agreed.

"I see you've lost your silver locket!"

Helen clutched at her breastbone. The locket with her mother's picture was not on its chain. "I think I dropped it in the *Whaler* office," she said. She tried to remember. The whole afternoon was such a blur. Helen recalled the cuff of the chino pants as clear as a photograph. Two threads hanging off. She remembered the white sweat sock, a burr stuck to it, the Nike sneaker with the *e* worn off, and the stump. The stump with the soft, black humus where she'd hidden. She knew she'd lost the locket there. "I'll check in the lost-and-found at school," she told Aunt Stella and went up and ran the water for her bath. There was no negative of her mother's picture. And the only print had been in the locket. The picture was one of her mother laughing. She loved it more than any other. Without it safely against her breastbone she felt curiously un-protected, as if someone could now do her harm.

Through the bathroom walls Helen heard her father arrive. She heard his conversation with Aunt Stella as an exchange of muffled grunts and high-pitched squeals about the rock thrower and the *Whaler*. She put on a fresh shirt and jeans and made sure she looked as clean, combed, and innocent as possible. The scratches were angrier than ever. They stung like bee bites from the water and soap. *If I had straight hair,* Helen decided, *I could brush a big swoosh of it over half the scratches on my face,* but of course she didn't have straight hair.

Her father took her into his arms and held a glass of beer around the small of her back while he hugged her. He was a compact man with bushy eyebrows, bushy hair, and baggy suits that always seemed to wrinkle and sag even before he came down in the mornings, no matter how many times Aunt Stella had them pressed. His life's work was a passion, carried out on behalf of the Massachusetts Department of Water Purification. For them he traveled the state, sampling water supplies for signs of toxic pollution. He railed against those industries and nameless dumpers that dared contaminate the drinking water of innocent citizens. "From me," he told Helen often, "you've got a head of wild hair and a heart on the side of the angels. Let us hope you've inherited your mother's caution and quiet ways."

This part of Helen's inheritance had not yet shown itself.

"Now, tell me," he said, kissing her on the forehead, "what's all this I hear about you tailing some bloody hellkite up a hill into the woods?"

"I wanted to see who it was, Dad. If he's the one who's

been throwing rocks at cars, the Punk Rock Thrower, I could have identified him. I could have—"

"You wanted to catch him, didn't you?" asked her father, smiling.

"Well, you should have seen the poor little girl and her mom. They were nearly killed."

"And so could you have been. A slip of a girl like you up in the woods with a psychopath twice your size." Her father held her close. "Promise never to do such a thing again?"

"Okay, Dad."

"You're all I have in the world. Remember that, Sweet Pea," he said.

"You've got me!" Aunt Stella snapped from the kitchen. Helen's father bent to pick a yellowed leaf off one of his geraniums in the window. "And I don't know what I'd do without you, Stella!" he called into the kitchen.

Aunt Stella answered him with "Dinner!"

Helen and her father walked arm in arm to the table. Her father said grace, and as they began slicing up Aunt Stella's rock-hard macaroni and cheese with steak knives, he winked and congratulated Helen on her new job at the *Whaler*. "Stella tells me you have to draw a picture for an ad, is it?"

"A Hummel figurine," said Helen. She got up and took the box out of her pocketbook. "Oh, *no*," she said. "It's chipped. The policemen must have banged it when they piled all our stuff on the edge of the highway. What am I going to do? It costs fifty dollars."

Helen's father picked up the figurine and examined it. The chip was right on the staff the little boy was holding.

"Ugly thing," he said, putting it down in disgust. "Ordinarily you'd have to pay for it yourself, but this was a good cause, babe. Stella, can you pick her up one just like it?"

"Please, Aunt Stella," Helen begged. "Barry de Wolf will kill me if he sees it's been broken."

"Who is Barry de Wolf?" asked Aunt Stella.

"Some senior," said Helen, "on the *Whaler*. He's the business manager, I think. His name's right under Jerry Rosen's on the masthead. Jerry's the editor, and he'll probably fire me from my new job. And then there's Beverly Boone. She's another senior. If she sees I've messed up on my first day, she won't ever let me help her with the paste-up. I don't have fifty dollars, Aunt Stella." Actually Helen did have forty-eight dollars. It was stashed away in the back of her closet. She was saving up until she had sixty dollars in hand, and then she intended to go out and have her hair straightened.

"Well," said Aunt Stella with an agreeable sigh, "it would be unwise to disappoint the people on the newspaper. They sound very nice, by the way. Young people with a future ahead of them. Unlike that weedy creature you brought in today with the dirty fingernails. He'll never amount to a hill of beans."

"That's not fair, Aunt Stella," said Helen. "Pinky Levy runs the printing press for the *Whaler*. His nails are inky, not dirty. Besides, he was terrific helping the mother and the little girl at the accident, and I like him."

"Who are you talking about?" asked Helen's father.

"Something that the cat dragged in," said Aunt Stella.

"Is that Sam Levy's boy?" asked Helen's father. "Skinny with freckles and a cowlick sticking up like an Indian feather?"

"His cowlick—" Helen began, but her father interrupted.

"He's all right, that kid. I took samples from the cistern near the motel they own. Mother's a widow. Sam died years ago. She's Swedish, I think. The Seafarer is a clean place, and the boy and the mother were very helpful."

"Motel!" said Aunt Stella. "Taking riffraff off the streets."

Helen did not stay to argue. She went to her room and finished as many of the homework assignments as were still legible on the crumpled papers she'd collected during the day's classes. Then she placed the Hummel figurine on her desk top and began to draw it.

Once Aunt Stella came up to say good night and to bring Helen a bowl of slightly melted frozen custard. She looked at the Hummel boy with admiration. "Let's hear him play," she said. "He's so adorable."

"No!" said Helen. "I can hardly stand looking at him, much less listening to one of those awful little tunes."

Her father came in for his kiss good night. He scrutinized her drawings. "Not your usual style, is it, Sweet Pea?" he asked. "Still and all, I suppose it may come in handy one day to know how to draw such a thing."

"Dad," said Helen, "if I sing you a song, can you tell me the name of it?"

"I might. If it's an Irish ballad, I might."

"It isn't. It goes like this." Helen began humming and

then singing the words she could remember from hearing the song many times. She did not try to whistle it as the man in the woods had done.

"Hm . . ." said her father. "That's . . . that's whatchamajiggy . . . 'The Happy . . .' 'The Happy Wanderer.' That's the name of it. Why do you ask?"

"Oh, I just heard it somewhere is all," she said airily. She looked into her father's intense blue eyes. He knew she wasn't telling him all of the truth, but he let it go and kissed her good night and tucked her in after her prayers were said, just as he had done when she was little.

Helen was very nearly asleep when the sound of the television downstairs in the living room woke her up. In seconds she was crouched on the landing listening to the late local news. "New Bedford area drivers can rest easily tonight for the first time in two months," the announcer droned. Helen positioned herself so she could just see his flickering face on the old black-and-white TV. "Since midsummer random rock throwings along Route Six outside of New Bedford have terrorized local drivers and resulted in several accidents. An intensive manhunt was called off tonight with the arrest of Duane 'Stubby' Atlas of Forty-two Dock Street, New Bedford. An anonymous tipster directed police to a bar in the wharf area. Atlas was found in possession of several grams of heroin. The latest incident occurred today, when Mrs. J. J. Sokol of Dartmouth and her young daughter narrowly missed death as a rock hit their car. Atlas is believed to have been under the influence of drugs at the time."

Helen's father turned off the TV and without looking up said, "I know you're there listening, Sweet Pea."

"Okay, Dad. I am," said Helen.

She could hear the smile in her father's voice. "Your worries are over," he said. "Thank God they got him."

"Yes, Dad."

"And to think you chased him, a near murderer, a drug addict, up through the woods. You promise me you'll never do anything so foolish again?"

"Yes, Dad."

"He went to St. Theresa's, the Atlas boy, didn't he?"

"Yes, Dad," she repeated automatically. "Three or four years ahead of me."

"You never know," said her father.

Helen tried to sleep, but sleep would not come. Over and over the song, whistled so beautifully, repeated itself. Over and over Helen came to the same flat certainty. It hadn't been Stubby she'd seen in the woods. Never in a hundred years would Stubby whistle that song.

FOUR

By Saturday morning Helen, sitting in her bedroom, had lost count of her drawings. She supposed she was up to sixty or seventy. On Wednesday and Thursday and then on Friday she had presented several to Jerry Rosen and Barry de Wolf. Too much expression in the eyes was their verdict each time. Not cute enough. Not round and dimpled and Hummelly enough. Maybe Beverly could do it. But Beverly was not interested in doing a drawing for free, now that she made a nice bit of money selling her caterpillar jewelry.

Helen sweated over her latest sketch and waited for Pinky to come and take her to the football game. She hated the Hummel music box more than ever. She hated Jerry and Barry for being so superior and rejecting her hateful drawings over and over again. She was grimly determined to get it right. She was sure Jerry and Barry and Beverly would be more respectful toward her if her hair were straight and her figure anything but pencillike.

As the morning hours passed, Helen's concentration dwindled. She began to doodle distractedly. In the back of her mind, taking wonderful turns and growing surely, was a whole new idea. The *Whaler* ran a weekly contest for the best story written by a student. At the end of the year the very best of these articles was given a gold medal. *If Barry de Wolf can win a gold medal with a sleep-inducing essay about the birds of New Bedford, then I can win it too,* she had decided. Her father had said it was a splendid idea. Aunt Stella had said it was not the right thing for a young girl to go chasing people up into the woods or to write about it either. Nonetheless, Helen had decided to do it and had announced her intention over breakfast the morning after the accident.

Surely, she thought, the other articles that she'd seen so far on a clipboard outside Jerry's office didn't hold a candle to hers. One was about growing potatoes under the sea. Another was entitled "Why I Want to Be a Teacher." Helen began trying out titles for her story. She was good at lettering. Earlier in the week she had thought of calling her story "Near Death for Mother and Baby." That sounded like a headline in the *National Enquirer* at the supermarket checkout. "Witness to an Accident" was too tame and boring. The story she had in mind would be light on the description of blood and gore and heavy on the part about chasing the rock thrower through the woods. She decided at last to call it "The Man in the

Woods." Her lettering was perfect. It looked printed. She smiled and daydreamed of the gold medal she would win. The story would be so good, she was sure it would win not only the gold medal but help earn the *Whaler* its state journalism prize. Then Jerry and Barry and Beverly would sit up and take notice of her. How sorry they would be that they had given her such a hard time. How admiring they'd have to be, squirming in their seats on Class Day when the principal called her name and handed her the gold medal. How grateful Jerry would be.

Aunt Stella pretended to be surprised when Pinky rang the doorbell. "Somebody here to see you!" her soprano voice called up the stairway.

Helen jumped and ran to the mirror. She pulled a hair-brush as vigorously as she could through her curls, trying, as always, to deny their existence. *I can't wait to get twelve more dollars saved,* she said angrily to herself. *I'm going to have my hair straightened and look like a normal human being for once instead of someone who stuck her hand in an electric socket.*

Pinky was doing his best to appear respectable to Aunt Stella. Helen could hear polite noises coming from him down in the living room. She could also hear Aunt Stella pacing, picking up her little knickknacks and dusting them off as she always did when she was nervous.

"I'm going to drive both of you to the stadium," Aunt Stella announced when Helen ran downstairs.

Helen saw Pinky's face fall slightly. "Oh, Aunt Stella," she said, "there's so much traffic. We'll take the bus like everybody else."

Aunt Stella settled her gaze on Pinky's cowlick, which

was coming slowly unstuck. Helen hoped she wouldn't attempt to fix it. "I have to pick up your new music box at Perry and Crowe anyway," said Aunt Stella, still looking at the cowlick. She prided herself on having a way with hair. Helen knew better than to argue.

During the ride to the stadium Aunt Stella recounted her favorite experiences from high school when she had been their age. This was bad enough, but the high school in Ireland had been called a grammar school, which somehow made things worse. She told them who had asked her to dance at the graduation ball. Helen closed her eyes. She'd heard the story many times before. Then Aunt Stella told them how difficult schools were back then. Everyone could recite from memory all thirty-six verses of "The Downfall of the Gael." Helen prepared her arguments for taking the bus home instead of being picked up after the game. What she wanted to do was to go back to the woods and look for her lost locket. She was sure it must have been torn off by a tree branch. Perhaps it had fallen off when she'd hidden under the stump. What she said she wanted to do was to have a soda with the rest of the kids from the *Whaler* after the game. Aunt Stella believed that having a soda with other clean-cut high school achievers was a step up the ladder of being popular, Helen knew. Pinky helped. "We'll just be about an hour at Howard Johnson's," he said encouragingly. No high school groups ever went to Howard Johnson's. They went to Vito's Time Warp or Pizza City. Aunt Stella could not think of a reply quickly enough. The car in back of them honked. Pinky and Helen leaped out and, fading into the crowd, yelled, "Good-bye!"

Aunt Stella, hopelessly caught in the snaking traffic, yelled back fortissimo, "Don't get into any strangers' cars!" over the honking horns behind her.

Most of the people pouring into the stadium entrances wore partisan colors, red and white for New Bedford, black and orange for Fall River. Chrysanthemums with ribbons in both combinations sold briskly at the sidewalk stands. The leaves on the elms that lined the street were turning yellow at the edges. The trees were dwarfed by the huge stadium. The stadium had been built many years ago and had been meant to look like a Roman coliseum. Helen decided to let herself be caught up in the spirit of the day. She never would have imagined, a week ago, that she would be at a football game with a boy, but here she was, with her drawing pad clasped tightly under her arm and the still summery air laced with the promise of autumn. She and Pinky found seats at the thirty-yard line on the New Bedford side, as close to the field as they could so that Helen would have a good view of the players. Helen apologized to Pinky for Aunt Stella's awful conversation.

"I don't mind," said Pinky. "Actually the conversation can get much worse at my house. Especially when my relatives from Norway visit us. They speak English and Norwegian, and of course I only speak English, so they feel all superior. They can't understand why my mom married an American. A Jewish American too. Since my dad's been dead, eight years, they've been pushing her to move back to Norway. They think she'll find some nice Norwegian widower to marry. Jeez Louise, that's all she needs. Some clown who manufactures frozen fish cakes next door to the North Pole. My relatives think it would be good for me and my sister to go to school there." Pinky made a noise as if he were spitting out vinegar. "My mom's plenty proud of me and my sister the way we are," he added. "Wednesday afternoon she sent the relatives the article from the paper."

Helen took the newspaper article from last Wednesday's *Post-Dispatch* out of her wallet. "DRUG-CRAZED ROCK THROWER TRACKED BY CLEVER COPS" was the headline. "Maniac with Bad Aim Sought to Loot Jewelry Trucks" was the subheadline. Helen read the whole thing over for the twentieth time.

> New Bedford police ended a two-month search and a two-month seige of terror for local residents with the arrest Tuesday night of Duane "Stubby" Atlas of 42 Dock Street. Police sources have suspected for some time that there was a pattern to the rock throwing. Their suspicions proved correct when they arrested a heroin addict and son of local mobster Chet Atlas. Atlas was aiming his rocks at the UPS delivery trucks that routinely carry merchandise for Perry and Crowe's huge mail order business. According to police sources he was hoping to cause an accident and loot the trucks of their jewelry and money. A spokesman for Perry and Crowe expressed horror at the incidents and informed this paper that all valuables, jewelry and cash, are shipped at irregular intervals in Brinks armored vans. "All this

madman could hope to do was take human life and smash up a little china and glass," said the spokesman.

Atlas has been charged with attempted murder, aggravated assault, and possession of heroin. His last victims, a mother and child from Dartmouth, were slightly injured Tuesday afternoon when Atlas hit their car instead of the UPS truck in front of them. Two local teenagers, Olaf Levy, 15, of Seafarer Way, and Mary Helen Curragh, 14, of Prospect Avenue, New Bedford, will be awarded good citizenship certificates by the Chamber of Commerce for giving first aid to the victims.

"Olaf Levy!" said Helen.

"Yeah, well," said Pinky, "I was named after my mom's father. Anyway, look who's talking, *Mary*."

Helen sighed. "Named after you know who," she said.

"What a record that Atlas guy had," said Pinky as they watched the football teams doing vigorous push-ups on the field. "Heard it over the radio. Petty larceny, possession of a knife, purse snatching, vandalism, drugs. Since he's been eight years old, that guy's been making trouble. They ought to drop him over Siberia at ten thousand feet."

Helen frowned. "I wonder," she said.

"You wonder what?"

"Oh, nothing." She tossed her head as if to rid herself of a thought too large to think. "I hope they got the right guy."

"Are you kidding?" Pinky asked. "They got Atlas dead

to rights! He was a crazy doped-up weirdo with a record a mile long. Can you just imagine what he'd have done to you if he'd found out you were following him up through the woods? Gives me the shakes just to think about it."

"I guess you're right," said Helen.

"Right? Right about what?"

"It must have been Stubby after all that I followed. It had to be. Anybody else would have helped us."

"So why should you think it wasn't him?"

"Just . . . the whistling. It didn't sound like him. 'The Happy Wanderer' doesn't sound like a song that a person like Stubby would know."

"Eh!" said Pinky. "He could have heard it on the Musak."

"Well, I hope they put him in jail for fifty years," said Helen, her eyes on one of the football players who was jogging in place. She sketched the player with quick, sure lines, fascinated by the straining, powerful muscles under the endless layers of tape, pads, and outsized plastic devices stuck under the shoulders of his shirt. The cheerleaders, bright-eyed and squeaky clean, leaping in their heavy white sweaters with red *N.B.*'s, urged the crowd to "Gimme an *N*! Gimme an *E*!" As she drew, Helen yelled back to them with Pinky and the rest of the crowd.

At half time the Fall River band worked its way out of the opposite side of the grandstand playing "Columbia the Gem of the Ocean." They formed a strange pattern at midfield which Helen could not identify until the PA microphone announced it was a diamond and the theme for the half-time entertainment was precious stones.

"You want a hot dog?" Pinky asked.

"Yes, sure," said Helen, and she followed him over the benches, down a set of granite steps, and into the darkness of the stadium's interior. "Your first football game?" Pinky asked.

"Yup," said Helen.

"Like it?"

"I do," she answered. "I didn't think I would. I hate it on television, and I only came to draw the booster tags, but it's fun!" Helen did not say *I wouldn't like it nearly so much if you weren't here with me*. She only thought that. They had reached the very back of the crowd that stood in the lines for the hot-dog concession. Pigeons and swallows nested high up in the secret hollows of the stone rafters. Every voice echoed to twice its volume in the cool darkness of the enormous granite arches.

"Wait here," shouted Pinky, and he began squeezing between people, working his way to the counter. Helen could see his cowlick bobbing up and down as he got closer to the front. Being with a boy at a football game had always been something she imagined happened to other people, like free trips to Hawaii. It was something that pretty, popular, normal girls did.

The crowds converged thickly at the tunnels which led back to the grandstand. Helen felt Pinky's hand close tightly around hers in the chilly gloom, three pushing girls going in different directions between herself and Pinky. It really didn't count as holding her hand of course. He was just trying to guide her through the crowd, and there was nothing romantic in both of them holding dripping hot dogs away from the bumping bodies. Still, she felt a peculiar lightness and happiness inside. She didn't want him to let go of her hand. Then she heard it.

Not far behind them someone was whistling, and her heart, or whatever it was in the middle of her that a minute before had felt like the inside of a star, now flopped over and turned to ice. Sweat beaded her whole body. Silvery, perfectly modulated notes, again like the tremulo of a flute, drifted over the clot of people chattering and pushing around her. Her hand slipped out of Pinky's, and she stood pinned until the crowd moved again. Pinned as she had been under the stump in the woods, listening to the same tune and the same whistler with her pulse rattling like a freight train and her mouth as dry as sand.

Pinky managed to grab her arm and pull her up the stairs to the daylight. "Listen!" she whispered. "Do you hear it? Do you hear it?"

"Hear what? What's the matter?"

"Listen!"

The whistling had gone off another way now, was lost somewhere in the vast inner ring of the stadium, but it could still be heard. Then it stopped.

Pinky scratched his ear. "Yes, I heard it," he said, "but it could have been anybody. Anybody could whistle that song."

"No. No. It was the same person. I've never in my life heard anyone whistle like that, Pinky. I want to find out who it was."

The kickoff for the second half sailed through the air. The press of people forced them down the steps and back into their seats. Pinky began wolfing down his hot dog.

Helen held hers in her lap, as if it had turned to stone. "I can't eat," she said. "I'm too scared."

"Well, what are you going to do?" asked Pinky. "You can't go prowling around the stadium waiting for somebody to start whistling."

"First of all," said Helen, "do you believe me?"

"Believe you?" he asked, evening out the mustard on his hot dog with one finger and wiping it on the underside of his jeans.

"Do you believe me that it's the same guy I heard in the woods?"

"I guess so. I mean, you looked like a ghost, and you told me about it right away. It's the same song for sure. You sang it to me. But what of it? Maybe it *is* the same guy. But maybe the cops were right. It was probably the Indian the policeman mentioned or a jogger, and he whistles nicely, and he's here at the game today. What of it?"

Helen's eyes followed the football players as they ran up and down the field, tumbling in heaps over one another. She had no recognition of what they were doing. "The Indian, a jogger, anyone else would have helped us out, Pinky. The only person who would have walked away from that accident is the guy who threw the rock. Stubby's in jail. The rock thrower is here at this game."

Pinky crumpled his hot-dog wrapper and dropped it between his feet. "Holy Christmas night," he said.

The only reminder of Tuesday's accident left on the highway was a swath of tiny ice-cube bits of broken glass. Helen coaxed some of it into a mound with her toe and squinted up the hill toward the woods.

"It'll be dark soon," said Pinky. "Are you sure you want to go up there? Just to find a locket?"

Wood asters, butterfly weed, and cornflowers, blue as the afternoon sky, danced innocently in the fallow light. Beyond the field were the scrub pines, their branches always half rotten and covered with hard lichen. As the hill rose, so did the height of the trees, until they became just a mass of faraway blackness, hiding ferns and rabbits, moss and mushrooms, like an endless attic filled with trinkets. And secrets.

"My mother's up there," said Helen. "I know it sounds silly. But I've always had that locket right up against me, ever since she died, and I look at it, at the picture, every night before I go to sleep. I know it's just a picture, but it's the only one of her I really love, and there's no negative. I don't want to . . . leave her up there all alone in those woods."

"Doesn't sound silly," said Pinky, and he jammed his hands in his pockets and led the way up the hill.

The woods were full of calling birds and twanging insects. She retraced her steps through the prickly scrub oaks and pines with their half rotting rough-barked timbers, which scratched like carpenters' rasps, but no silver locket gleamed from a branch or from the weed-covered ground. They found the stump, and Helen poked through the soft black earth under it. Again no locket. There was a rustling, suddenly, in the bushes near a stream up the hill where she'd lost sight of the whistler.

They saw a man, and he saw them. Helen jumped. Then she realized this old limping man was nothing like the person she had followed.

In his hand was a white plastic milk jug. He had apparently been collecting water from the stream. He was quite old, and many inches over six feet tall, with a face as wizened in wrinkles as a walnut shell. He limped a few steps toward them and then stood staring.

"We didn't mean to bother you," said Helen as cheerfully as she could.

"I heard ja coming," said the old man. "What are you looking for?"

"Just a lost silver locket," said Helen.

"How'd you lose a silver locket up here?" he asked suspiciously. He set his jug down, knelt on one knee, and clasped the other with enormous brown, veiny hands. "Nothing up here. 'Cept the water."

"Water?" asked Pinky.

"Good for the blood," said the old man. "Town water's no good. Full of chemicals. I drink this here for my rheumatism. Bad knee." He wiped some pine needles off the wet bottom of his milk jug, sniffed, and went on. "So I told you how come I'm here. You tell me how come you lost a piece of jewelry a half mile from the highway."

"It's a long story," said Helen.

"Got more time than money," said the old man.

So Helen told him—with Pinky adding a few flourishes to her story—of the accident and the chase up the hill.

"Cops didn't like your story?" he asked when she'd gotten to the part about the policeman in the house.

"They wouldn't even listen," said Helen.

"Cops!" The old man laughed gently. "I stay away from 'em. They find me, they'll nip me off into one of those nursing homes in town."

"Not against your will, they couldn't," said Helen stoutly.

The old man laughed again. "I'm an Indian," he said. "Wampanoag from the islands. Cops don't like Indians. I live on public land. Against the law. I work a bit. Different jobs. I got a nice little place to live in, but nobody knows where it is. I don't bother the cops, and the cops don't bother me. I saw one of the rocks go flying out and hit the fender of a truck. Maybe two months back. Never told the cops. Truck kept right on going. Never made the papers."

"But the rock could have killed someone," said Helen.

"Lots of things kill people," said the Indian with a caved-in smile. Helen guessed he had no teeth. "Course, if I'd been up here Tuesday like you and seen the accident and all, that would have been different. Least I'd have put a tourniquet on the lady. You're brave kids. Good hearts, helping the lady and the kid. Stupid to chase that guy, though." He shook his head in wonderment. "You never know. You should stay out of these woods, kids. Stay out," he repeated in a sad voice with a crooked finger raised like a schoolteacher's.

"I think we'll go home now," said Helen. A north wind had begun rustling through a stand of immense junipers beyond where they stood. Clouds blew over the sun, chilling her further. She wished she'd brought a sweater.

"You the young fellow who owns that cracked-up old motorbike I see hiding in the shed down there?" asked the Indian.

"How did you know about that?" said Pinky.

"I know everything and I see everything in these

woods," was the chuckling answer. "If I spot that locket of yours, miss, I'll drop it in one of the saddlebags on the bike." He struggled to his feet and, slipping an index finger through the handle of his water jug, turned to walk away. "Don't you tell no cops you've been talking to me," he said. "Don't want them up here finding me, putting me in a rest home to die."

"I promise," said Helen.

The Indian smiled and limped slowly into the brush, blending with it, as quietly as a cat.

Neither Pinky nor Helen spoke until they had reached Pinky's hidden bike and had ridden it almost to the edge of Prospect Avenue. Pinky stopped the bike. "Good-bye," he said. "I have to get home. Saturday nights I have to take the desk of the motel. We get over twenty people and my mother has to run back and forth to the rooms to cover complaints—kid's cribs, extra pillows—you name it. We're not exactly a Holiday Inn. See you tomorrow. Remember, we gotta hit the books for the history test Monday."

"About one?" asked Helen. "After church?" She got off the motorbike and snapped shut the flaps of a saddlebag that had been rubbing uncomfortably against her leg. The snap reminded her of something. It was bronze, with the insignia of the old German Army, an eagle. She fretted over it a moment. It was something like . . . like what? Like the eagle on the necklace that Stubby had been twirling around and Mr. Casey had snatched away from him, accusing him . . . "Pinky," said Helen.

"What's the matter?"

"Tuesday afternoon I saw Stubby for just a minute or

two in Mr. Casey's office. Mr. Casey was yelling at him for stealing a necklace from a Perry and Crowe truck. I heard Mr. Casey say loud and clear that Stubby had a summer job loading trucks for Perry and Crowe."

Pinky picked a long shaft of barley grass and sucked on it between his two front teeth.

"Well, I knew Stubby a little from back in St. Theresa's. He wasn't stupid. If he had a job loading UPS trucks, he'd know what he was loading in the trucks, wouldn't he? If he was trying to support his drug habit by stealing jewelry or money, he'd have tried to rob the store instead. He certainly wouldn't waste his time throwing rocks at UPS vans carrying knickknacks. What's he going to do? Cause an accident, run out on the highway, and make off with a pair of Lenox teacups? And sell 'em for dope on a street corner? He *had* to know what went into the trucks. He *worked* there."

Pinky chewed the grass stem to bits and threw it away.

"Pinky, I *heard* him, and it wasn't Stubby. I *saw* him, and it wasn't Stubby. Stubby walks like an ape. Whoever this was walks gracefully. And now the police are saying Stubby was out there trying to loot jewelry trucks. That's ridiculous. I don't believe it. Do you?"

Pinky sucked a new piece of grass. Very slowly, his eyes never leaving Helen's, he shook his head.

"Pinky," said Helen. "No matter what the cops say, I've seen another part of this crime, haven't I?"

FIVE

After church Aunt Stella, who had been working on it for most of the morning, still could not come up with a good reason for Helen not to help Pinky with his history homework. "Doing homework is something you do with a friend, not a boy," she insisted.

"But Pinky *is* a friend," Helen insisted also.

Aunt Stella agreed at last to allow this to happen if it was to be "just this once." "According to Martha Malone," she said, "he's a good boy. He helps his mother out at that motel she owns." Aunt Stella pronounced the word *motel* as if she meant gambling den. "Martha also says he's been held back a year in school."

"Only one year," said Helen. "That doesn't matter much."

"It may not matter now, Helen," Aunt Stella warned, "but it will matter later. Martha says he's a poor student. You never know when there's some minimal brain damage. Those things are carried on from generation to generation."

"Aunt Stella, please," said Helen. "I'm not getting married to him. I'm just doing some homework with him."

Aunt Stella sighed. "Just so you don't think of him as someone with a future ahead of him," she answered.

Even though Aunt Stella was completely prepared for Pinky's arrival, she trilled, "Somebody here to see you!" up the stairs to Helen's room when Pinky arrived.

They sat in the overstuffed wrought-iron lounges on the screen porch. For twenty minutes Helen read Pinky her notes about the Battle of Saratoga. Once again Pinky had slicked back his hair with water. His cowlick was just beginning to come to life on the back of his head. Several times he looked nervously in the direction of the kitchen, where Aunt Stella was making pleasant humming noises with an appliance.

"What's she cooking in there?" Pinky asked when they'd finished studying.

"Don't ask," said Helen. "Pinky, we have to go back to the police."

"No."

"Yes."

"No way. They weren't interested before. They won't be interested now. No way."

"Pinky, please listen."

"No."

"Will you at least listen?"

"I'll listen, but—"

"Just hear me out. First of all, I'm going to write a story for the *Whaler*. I'm going to write about everything. The accident. Chasing the guy through the woods. And I'm going to end the story on one big fat question. How come Stubby was trying to rob UPS trucks when he *had* to know all Perry and Crowe's valuables were shipped in Brinks vans? I'm going to get a gold medal for my story, Pinky, but I have to find out whatever more I can from the cops."

"Number one," Pinky began, "the cops will absolutely not listen. Number two, Jerry Rosen will never in a hundred years even print your story. The stories that win the prizes are always about looking for fossils in Springfield Quarry or . . . or teaching handicapped kids. The stories are judged by a bunch of teachers, and that's the kind of thing teachers like. Not crime stories. No way you're going to get that gold medal."

"Pinky, nobody's ever tried a story like this before, I'll bet a million bucks. But *I'm* going to try, and I'm going to win it. You wait. The Punk Rock Thrower's been terrorizing drivers for two months. It's been all over the local papers and TV. If I can show that maybe the cops arrested the wrong guy, not only will it be in the *Whaler,* it'll be in the *Post-Dispatch* too. Pinky, it'll be a real story, not just some boring thing about bird-watching. It's a one hundred percent cinch."

"No freshman's ever won the gold medal," said Pinky.

"That's going to change," Helen answered.

Pinky picked up a loose bit of mortar and stuck it back

between two pieces of slate on the floor of the porch. "I hate cops," he said.

"I want to see their files," said Helen. "Don't worry. I'm not going to go marching in telling them they were wrong. I just want to see their files and ask them why they arrested Stubby. Will you come?"

Pinky didn't answer this. He was busy with his bits of mortar.

"Pinky, do you think that in the twentieth century, in Massachusetts, U.S.A., the cops should arrest the wrong guy?"

Pinky did answer this, after a long wait. "All right," he said miserably, "but don't expect anything from the cops. They wouldn't tell us if the atom bomb fell."

"Believe me," said Helen, "Aunt Stella will be a lot tougher than the cops."

"The police station!" said Aunt Stella when they went into the kitchen to tell her they were going. Her hands were covered with gray, sticky dough. "Why on earth do you want to go to the police station?"

"It's my story for the *Whaler,* Aunt Stella."

"I thought you were an artist, not a writer."

"Aunt Stella, we won't be long, I promise."

"*We?* First you and now him?"

"Pinky's helping me, Aunt Stella."

Aunt Stella shook the dough off her fingers into a bowl with a violent gesture. "I thought *you* were helping *him,*" she said.

"We finished the homework. What harm could come to us at the police station?"

"I was just making you some nice crullers," said Aunt Stella.

"We'll be home in time to eat them hot out of the oven," Helen answered as reassuringly as she could.

"I don't know what your father would say. He'll be back from the store in an hour."

"Daddy'd be proud of me, Aunt Stella. He liked the idea of the story. Just think. Me a lowly freshman winning a gold medal for the first time in the history of the *Whaler*!"

"You have your father's silver Irish tongue, that's what you have," said Aunt Stella.

"Aunt Stella, you're as Irish as Daddy."

"Yes, and most of my Irish rubbed off on my poor Yankee husband, who drank himself to death, God rest his soul. I'm an American citizen, thank you very much." Helen held in what her father always said when Aunt Stella denied her Irishness: She can take an oath, change her name, and sign a piece of paper, he had told Helen many times when Aunt Stella was out of earshot, but she'll never change her cooking, her temper, or her religion, and they're as Irish as Paddy's pig, so there. "Please, Aunt Stella," Helen begged.

"I don't know what your poor dead mother would think," Aunt Stella began but Pinky cut in, "I'll take care of her," he said.

"You!" said Aunt Stella. "She's got twice your brains even if she's half your size!"

When they'd gotten a few paces down the sidewalk, Helen stopped. "Pinky, I'm so sorry about what she said. I'm so embarrassed."

"Eh!" Pinky answered her airily. "Don't worry about it. Relatives are relatives. My relatives think I'm stupid too. They can't believe I got kept back a year in an American school. If I went to school in Norway, they tell me, I'd have to learn three languages and differential calculus by seventh grade. They always tell me if I ate more fish like they do up in Norway, I'd get straight A's. Eat fish, be smart, and live to a hundred. That's what my Aunt Sonja tells me every time she comes over."

"Do they live to a hundred?"

"Nah," said Pinky. "They freeze to death first."

Helen began to laugh.

"What are you laughing at?" Pinky asked, laughing himself.

"Just grown-ups. I hope when I'm a grown-up, my brain won't turn to solid rock like theirs."

Pinky stopped walking abruptly. Helen turned around and waited for him to say something. He looked suddenly embarrassed. Clumsily he touched Helen on the shoulder. "Cops are grown-ups with rock-hard ideas too," he said, "but I'm with you on this thing about the rock thrower. We'll do it together."

Chief Ryser was a big man, with enormous broad shoulders, a bull-like neck, and tiny, shiny little shoes. His smile twitched boyishly, and he seemed immensely pleased with himself and his spacious office. When Helen showed him her *Whaler* button, he was even more delighted and told them, "I'm an old *Whaler* man myself! Class of '43. Sports photographer. Had a bum knee so I couldn't play football. Now, what can I do for you nice folks?"

"We're doing an article, sir, for the *Whaler*," Helen began. "It's on the fine work of the New Bedford police." She swallowed hard knowing she wasn't off to a very convincing start. "This is Mr. Pinky Levy, who is helping me."

Ryser smiled like a crocodile.

"You see, sir, one of our classmates was arrested. That's Stubby Atlas, of course. We at the *Whaler* feel that his story should be an example to all other teenagers who think of taking drugs."

"Certainly should," said Chief Ryser. Another policeman moved quietly about in the corner of the office. Helen did not look directly at him, but she recognized him from the day of the accident. He had been in the house but hadn't talked to them.

"Could you tell us, sir," she asked Ryser, "a little about how you found it was Stubby throwing rocks and terrifying all those innocent drivers? We in high school really have so little idea of how the police work." Helen could nearly hear Pinky's thoughts quivering as he shifted uncomfortably in his chair. She wished he would sit still. Every time he squirmed, Ryser looked at him.

"Bring me the Atlas file, Frank," said Chief Ryser.

His eyes twinkled, and he grinned at Pinky and Helen when the manila folder was placed on his blotter. "A hundred-percent certified criminal, your classmate," he said. He licked his index finger and opened the file. "Here's a photo of what we found on him. That's ten grams of heroin. Cut, of course, but worth an arm and a leg. Some of these junkies will shoot up anything. This stuff was strong, let me tell you. Most of the time they're down to about five percent heroin. This stuff was almost ten. No wonder he almost OD'd."

"OD'd?" asked Helen.

"Overdosed. He had enough in him to kill an ox. If we hadn't gotten the tip-off note about him we did that night, he'd have been a goner."

"Tip-off note?" asked Helen, writing this on her drawing pad.

"Yup. About six P.M. Somebody dropped it in an empty squad car on the front seat. Car was parked at the corner of Wharf Street and Broad. We had that, and here . . ." He pushed a glossy photograph across the desk toward Helen.

"What's that?" she asked.

"On the left," he explained, "is an enlargement several thousand times of iron fragments found under Atlas's fingernails. You can see in this other photograph they match exactly the iron fragments from the rock that hit Mrs. Sokol's car."

"And the tip-off note, sir? It wasn't a telephoned tip-off?"

Ryser handed her the note. "Anybody who doesn't want to have his voice recorded won't call the station," he said. "They know we can take voice prints if we send the tape up to Boston. The fellow just dropped this in the squad car. We've seen it a hundred times. Guy who tipped us off was one of Atlas's pals, ninety-nine to one. Atlas was probably bragging his head off in a bar, some other jerk was listening, had a grudge, and told us about it.

Sometimes the police are lucky that way," he said with an ironic smile.

"Voice prints!" Pinky interrupted.

"Nothing but the best," said Ryser.

"I was looking at your new copying machine over there," Pinky remarked. "We sure could use one of those in the *Whaler* office. Save us a pile of work on the old mimeograph we have."

Ryser left his desk and went over to the copier. "Expensive model." He laughed out loud. "Taxpayers' expense. Still, it's a beaut, isn't it?"

Helen began reading the rest of the file on Stubby Atlas. The knees of his pants had been examined by experts and the grass stains and soil found in the fabric matched the soil and grass of the hillside overlooking the last accident.

Ryser turned back to Helen. "We sure got our man," he said, grinning.

"I guess so," Helen answered him. "Iron fragments under the fingernails, footprints. Positive identification by one of the victims—"

"And a confession," Ryser added proudly.

"A confession?" Helen asked.

"Signed and sealed," said Ryser. He paused and looked at her curiously. "Don't tell me you were the kids who were at the scene of the last accident."

"Yes," said Helen.

"You're the girl who said she saw somebody up there in the woods singing? The sergeant told me about it."

"Whistling," Helen answered, embarrassed. "And it wasn't Stubby Atlas either, because—"

"Honey," said Ryser sweetly, "of course it wasn't Stubby Atlas. You saw some jogger. Or maybe the old Indian living in the woods, I don't know. But what does it matter? Just look at this. This is a confession. Atlas signed it. He confessed to throwing the rocks at the trucks. Atlas's mother came and signed it too and told us to put her own son away like we put his old man away. She was disgusted with him. She herself told him God was going to spit on his grave for what he'd done. Atlas spent the whole night in jail kissing the priest's shoes and hands, asking forgiveness, thanking God he hadn't killed the baby and the mother. Now, you kids definitely get a good citizenship award for your help, but don't go thinking we caught the wrong guy."

"I don't think that . . . anymore," said Helen.

Ryser pulled on the lapels of his uniform jacket and smoothed down his hair, as if there had been a disturbance in the room.

"I should think not," he said. "You better not write some half-cocked tripe in the *Whaler* about us getting the wrong guy. I happen to know the Rosen boy, the editor. Responsible fellow too. He certainly isn't going to print anything against the police."

"I wasn't *against* the police," said Helen. "It's just . . ." She took in a deep breath and blurted out: "I don't believe that story in the *Post-Dispatch* about him throwing rocks at the trucks to loot them, sir. He worked for Perry and Crowe over the summer loading UPS trucks. He had to know they were full of worthless knickknacks."

"Where did you get that information?" asked Ryser stiffly.

"Well, last Tuesday I couldn't open my locker . . . never mind. Anyway, I was in the principal's office, and he was yelling at Stubby, and he said Stubby had a summer job loading trucks for Perry and Crowe."

Ryser fiddled with his cuff. "Okay," he said. "You are an observant young lady. Remember this. The police are not responsible for what goes into the newspapers. We just do our work." He straightened the other cuff. "When Mr. Richard Perry, who owns Perry and Crowe, found out we'd arrested Atlas, he went to his brother, Mr. John Seward Perry, who happens to own the *Post-Dispatch*. He told him to kill the story of Atlas working for Perry and Crowe. Bad for business. Actually we're guessing Atlas just wanted revenge on Perry and Crowe. Smash up their shipments—lots of glass all over the road. After all, they fired him. Found him trying to break in one night. Mr. Perry didn't want it in the papers that the store ever hired a jelly-brain like Atlas. Customers wouldn't like it. The little old ladies who buy their Christmas trinkets at Perry and Crowe might get the idea that more Atlases were lurking behind the counter, ready to wait on them. It was bad for the store image, so it didn't go in the papers. The Perrys own half this town. Everyone knows that."

"Oh," said Helen in a small voice. "He was just out there . . . for kicks? To get back at the store for firing him?"

Ryser nodded. "Any other questions?"

Helen and Pinky shook their heads, but in Helen's mind a warning light began to blink, and with the stubbornness of a metronome a shrewd voice whispered, *Something's wrong here. Something's wrong.*

"Now, I'll see those good citizenship awards get mailed to your houses. Look real pretty up on the wall. Come see us any time. Just remember, the Atlas case is closed. Thank God. Most of 'em don't work out so clean and easy." He glanced at his file. "Good luck with your article," he said. "By the way, young man, I'll just take that copy you made of the tip-off note. Confidential material!"

Pinky handed it over.

The other policeman followed them out into the hallway, at first, Helen thought, out of courtesy, but then she saw him beckon to them. He sat them down in a very different sort of office from the chief's. Blue paint peeled in layers off the walls and the radiator. Cigarette butts covered the floor. The policeman sat himself down behind a lame table and looked at his steeple-positioned fingers and then at Pinky and Helen with pain in his eyes. "I have a girl your age," he said, nodding toward Helen. "If anything happened to Lisa"—here he spread his hands, and they trembled a little—"I don't know what I'd do. I don't think I could go on living. Do you understand that?"

Pinky and Helen nodded.

"I was out at the house the day of the accident. Remember? You only saw me for a second when I poked my head in the door. But I heard you, young lady." He waited until he caught Helen's eye. "Yes, you," he went on. "Now, don't get me wrong. You're both great kids. Go write your article for the *Whaler*. But stop there. Don't go messing around anymore. This is heavy drugs. Atlas had a particularly fine grade of heroin on him. We don't know where it came from, but we're looking. We've got an eye on every dealer and junkie in New Bedford and Fall

River. You don't want to put one more toe in this cess-pool. Got it?"

"Yes," said Helen.

Pinky just stared ahead wide-eyed. Then Pinky said, "Can I ask you something?"

"You better. I want to answer every question in your hot little heads so you don't go poking around after the answers."

"The tip-off note?" Pinky said slowly. "The one that was dropped in the squad car?"

"Yeah? What about it?"

"The print on it. The typeface. I know something about printing. My Uncle Max is a printer. It was funny. Raised lettering almost like embossing . . . like a wedding invitation."

"Yeah. We tried to trace that. Probably some toy printing set. Maybe a foreign-make typewriter. We checked out every lead we could on that. But who cares? It was just some pea-brained pal of Atlas's who heard him bragging in a bar. Look, kids, we're not the FBI. This isn't a murder case involving some rich heiress from Newport or some rich doctor from Scarsdale. This is dangerous, workaday drug stuff, and the Atlas case is closed."

Helen looked questioningly at the officer's intent, tight face. Pinky scratched his stomach nervously.

"I want to tell you something," the officer went on. "Atlas's old man, Chet, is cooling his heels for fifteen years in Springfield State Prison. Drug pushing. Okay? Chet Atlas had a little red book with all the names and addresses of his contacts, other pushers all over the country. Okay? Now, he gave that little red book to his son,

Stubby, before we nabbed him. So what happens? Stubby Stupid loses the book. Fell out of a hole in his pocket, he says. He's terrified somebody whose name is in that book is going to find out he lost it. Stubby won't tell us anything about his old man's book or his old man's connections. He confessed to throwing the rocks and that's all. Now a lot of people are looking for that little red book, kids, including us. So you guys stay out of this. You don't want to run into some of Chet Atlas's pals, do you?"

"No!" said Helen.

"Good. Now, if I hear that you, young lady, take one more step playing detective, I'm going to tell your folks, and they'll keep you under lock and key at home for a year. As for you, Levy, I'll have that motorbike of yours taken away tomorrow. Understand?"

Pinky reddened and nodded.

"I don't want to see either of you at the Pearly Gates for another eighty years. Okay?"

At the bus stop, under the orange leaves of a sugar maple, Pinky breathed in a deep draught of the warm September air. "The end, my friend. Can't afford to lose my wheels."

"How did they know about your motorbike?" Helen asked.

"Cops have ears on every tree," Pinky answered morosely.

Helen gave a short, neat sigh. "Well, I'm glad it was Stubby who threw the rocks after all. Can you imagine, though, Pinky? The *Post-Dispatch* didn't print the whole truth? They left out the part about Stubby being an employee of Perry and Crowe? I'm going to end my

Whaler story with that fact. That's worth a gold medal."

The bus chugged into view at the end of the street. Pinky shuffled his feet impatiently. "Yes, well," he said at last, "I guess it was a jogger after all that you chased. Someone who didn't want to get involved."

"It must have been," said Helen. For an instant their eyes met guiltily. Helen knew Pinky didn't believe this any more than she did. "Pinky, I'm not going home right now," she said. "I want to visit one of my teachers from last year at St. Theresa's."

"Include me out," said Pinky. The bus pulled up and stopped in front of them. "Got a souvenir for you," Pinky announced cheerfully. He reached into his pocket and handed Helen a Xerox copy of the tip-off note.

"But Pinky! Ryser took the copy away from you!"

"I made three," said Pinky. "One for me, one for you, and one for him to take back." He jumped onto the bus, and with an explosion of smelly black exhaust the bus pulled out, leaving Helen waving from the sidewalk while Pinky waved from the window. Then he was gone. Helen wished she'd gone with him.

"He'd make a great thief," Helen explained to Sister Ignatius Paul over tea, "if he didn't have such a good streak inside him."

Sister Ignatius laughed. She took in Helen's eyes with her own big green ones. "A bit early, I think, my dear young child, for you to have such strong feelings for a boy."

Helen felt herself blush wildly. "I don't. Really, Sister. Pinky's just a friend."

"My dear child, I have asked you about everything under the sun concerning school and your family and the splendid story you intend to write, and you persist in talking only about this young man."

"But I *don't* have strong feelings, Sister. It's just that Pinky has been with me in this whole . . ."

"It is completely normal, I assure you. But one must never lose perspective. Never forget, Helen, the great gift that God has given you. In your drawing one day, you will speak in His voice, because it is His voice that speaks in you. Always remember that His gift is far more important than the strong tides of mortal ferment that are common to all of us, including, dear Lord forgive me, the most butterfingered girl at the A&P cash register whose imagination runs constantly to movie magazines."

Sister Ignatius adjusted the sleeves of her long, old-fashioned habit. All the other sisters in the order wore the lighter modern dress which Sister Ignatius had more than once called "street clothes." She claimed that much mystery and grace was lost in the wearing of street clothes, particularly the blocky blue twill suits that the Sisters of Mercy had selected. "Mother Luke does not argue with me," Sister Ignatius had also told Helen more than once. "If I don't want to teach school looking like a mortician's wife, I don't have to." Helen did not wonder at Mother Luke, because no one ever successfully argued with Sister Ignatius.

"Sister Ignatius," Helen insisted, holding her teacup as if it might fly from her hand, "I am not . . . I am not in love with Pinky Levy! And that's the truth!"

Sister Ignatius smiled mischievously under the spotless

black of her coif. "Dear," she said, "today is Sunday. By Monday you will think you are. Be warned! Now. Tell me more about the marvelous adventure you've had chasing after the Punk Rock Thrower! Tell me about the story you're going to write!"

"The adventure's all over," said Helen. "I've told you all there is to tell, right up to today, when we went to the police. I was so *sure* that it wasn't Stubby up in the woods, Sister. But I guess I was wrong. I must have been. It certainly was Stubby Atlas who threw those rocks out onto the highway. The police have proof. He confessed. Even his mother knows he's guilty. One of the police officers told us to stay clear of any more involvement. He threatened to tell my dad and Aunt Stella. He said he'd take Pinky's motorbike away if we went one more inch into this."

"A shame you can't do any more research," said Sister Ignatius. "I love adventures. But it's just as well. I'm sure you would only come to harm if you were to persist. Wouldn't it be something," she said abruptly, interrupting her own train of thought, "if we could just send this empty tea tray back on that trolley up there all the way to the kitchen and have them zip us out a new one!" She pointed upward to an old railing far up on the wall. "Did you know this convent was once New Bedford's first hospital? I've looked into it. There are all sorts of plans and old physicians' papers left in the basement. That, for example, was a patients' food trolley track. They were able to serve up to twenty meals on the trolley. Manually cranked from the kitchen, but still ingenious." Sister Ignatius had described the patients' food trolley on every single one of Helen's visits.

"Aunt Stella will be worrying about me," said Helen. "She'll probably call the police again if I don't get home."

"Of course, dear. And I have papers to correct. Don't worry your aunt. I understand she is a trial to you at times, but she has a good heart."

Helen kissed Sister good-bye on both cheeks. "And do take the policeman's advice," said Sister Ignatius. "Don't involve yourself in this any further."

"I won't," said Helen. "Look!" She reached into her pocketbook and withdrew Pinky's copy of the tip-off note. "This is enough to scare me to pieces every time I read it. I think I'll pin it over my desk just to remind myself to keep out of trouble."

Sister Ignatius propped a pair of exquisite gold-rimmed glasses, unlike the other nuns' steel-rimmed glasses, on the bridge of her nose. She read the note over at least three times. "Extraordinary!" she announced and gave it back to Helen. Helen read it again, frowning.

TO THE POLEESE:

STUBBY ATLAS, 42 DOCK STREET, NEW BEDFORD, IS THE TOILET HEAD FREEK WHO THROWED THEM ROKS AT CARS. I DONT WANT THAT HE NOWS WHO I AM BE-KAUZE HE MITE KILL ME OR MY SISTER. (YOU KAN FINE HIM TOONIHGT IN THE BAR AT THE DRIF INN ON THE WARF.)

"Clever job," said Sister Ignatius.

"Clever?" asked Helen. "It's awful!"

"Oh, yes, but dear heart, I have not been a teacher for twenty-five years for nothing. The grammar is appalling, the spelling is cretinous, but look at the punctuation!"

Helen stared at the words on the page. "It's all . . . correct," she said after a moment.

"Sublimely correct," said Sister Ignatius, removing her elegant spectacles and placing them deep in a recess in the mysterious folds of her habit. "A-plus work. *No* student who ever passed through the doors of my classroom who spelled and parsed his grammar as poorly as that ever punctuated like an English professor. Correct form of address, colon, spaces after commas and full stops, parentheses, and even a hyphen placed at the syllable break. What a pity you've squeezed the last drop of attention from our noble police force, because there is an educated mind behind that dreary note. He was just a little bit too well educated to convince a teacher. Good-bye, my dear child."

SIX

Armed with her Hummel figurine drawings, which Aunt Stella said were just adorable and which made Helen a little sick, and her football player drawings, which Helen was truly proud of, Helen raced down to the *Whaler* office at Monday's three o'clock bell. She peeked around Jerry Rosen's partition.

Jerry's telephone kept ringing. Freshmen pattered in and out with booster tag receipts and sophomores with copy for the next week's ads. Helen wondered if she would ever feel a part of all this. Her privileged position on the *Whaler*, as an indirect result of Mr. Bro's blackmailing Jerry, had not helped. Everyone was still a stranger to her. At last Jerry noticed her. "You do it right this time?" he asked.

"I hope so," answered Helen, feeling very much in the way.

Jerry stood and yelled, "Barry! Barry, where are you? This office is too crowded," he added. "Let's look at your drawings where there's some room."

Jerry and Beverly, phlegmatic and snapping her gum as usual, stared at the drawings which Jerry placed on an empty desk. At least ten other people milled around the desk, looking at Helen's Hummel drawings. Barry was playing poker in a corner, and he seemed annoyed at the idea of leaving the neat stack of nickels he had won. Several voices said, "Super! Really excellent," but Jerry paid them no attention. "Barry, what do you think?" he asked.

At this moment, with everyone looking on and complimenting her, Helen decided to place her football player pictures on the desk as well. More compliments were muttered. Jerry's telephone kept ringing. He looked over his shoulder in irritation at it and instructed Penny Parker to pick it up. "If it's the compositor," he yelled, "tell him I'm dead. Tell him he has to remake those plates because it was his fault and he knows it. Barry, come over here," he went on. "Take a look at this little German doll."

"How are the football players?" Helen asked confidently.

"They're okay," said Jerry, and Helen's heart rose expectantly. "But there's too much expression in the faces. Bev, get copies of these drawings. White out the faces and draw 'em in right."

"But . . . but you can't do that!" said Helen. "You can't have one person draw the body and another person draw the face."

"It isn't the football look," Jerry replied seriously. "You won't sell booster tags with football players looking like they just saw Frankenstein."

"But that's how they look!" Helen protested. "That's just what their faces do look like when they're catching the ball or kicking or passing. They grunt and groan and put everything into it, and their faces *do* look like that."

"Don't *whine*," said Jerry. "Bev, take care of these drawings. Barry, how about this German music box picture?"

Barry picked up his nickels. Sauntering over to the desk, he jingled them in his hand and said, "Better, but still too much expression in the eyes. I think Bev is going to have to do it. Mr. Perry can't wait much longer."

"Pay me, Barry," said Beverly.

"You know Mr. Perry has to have the drawing free, Beverly," Barry argued. "Be a team player, Beverly."

"Phoo to you, Barry de Wolf," said Beverly, and Helen admired her courage because she would have given the earth at that moment to say the same thing. Instead she collected her drawings and, telling herself sternly that this was the worst possible moment and that she should keep her mouth shut, said, "Jerry, I have an idea!"

"You have a lot of ideas," Jerry answered, backing toward his office door.

"May I just tell you what it is?" Helen kicked herself inwardly for the urgency in her voice.

"Friendly Jerry listens to everyone," he said, rolling up a wayward sleeve just so.

"I want to enter the *Whaler*'s contest for the best story. It's a true story, Jerry. It's about the Punk Rock

Thrower." Helen gulped hard and kept going. "You see, I was there, Pinky Levy too, the day the last accident happened. . . ."

"I saw it in the paper," said Jerry. "Both of you guys are getting good citizenship awards. So write it. I have no objection." He began backing away again.

"But that's not it," said Helen. "I don't want to write about being a good citizen. I want to write about Stubby Atlas and whoever tipped off the cops. I can prove that the *Post-Dispatch* lied and covered up the fact that Stubby worked at Perry and Crowe this summer. Mr. Perry didn't want that in the papers because he thought it would hurt the store's image. So his brother didn't print it. That's . . . that's fraud! Or something. There was someone else in the woods too, Jerry—I followed him. Anyway, if you like—"

"I don't like it," said Jerry. "Barry! Where are you? Barry, will you please tell Nancy Drew here what will happen to the *Whaler*'s advertising money if she starts spreading stories about Mr. Perry lying in the press."

Barry looked up from his cards. "He'll take his ads out of the *Whaler* pronto," said Barry.

"Look," Jerry went on with false patience, "I don't know why you want to cause so much trouble for the *Whaler*."

"I don't want to cause trouble. . . ." Helen answered.

"The *Whaler* isn't the *Police Gazette*," said Jerry.

"Trouble," said Barry. He put his cards down. Jerry steered Helen into a corner. Barry followed. Across the room Beverly was flirting with a freshman, giggling and making a fish mouth at him.

"First of all," Jerry said, his eyes on Beverly, "you've

got to get it into your head that this is a conservative, respectable newspaper. We want a state journalism award this year. We're not going to get it with left-wing cartoons, and we're not going to get it with stories about—"

"Let me talk to her, Jerry," Barry interrupted. "Look, she's going to cry if you keep at her. Just cool your jets, okay?" Barry sat and crossed his legs. "Helen," he said. "Is that it? Helen or Ellen?"

"Helen," said Helen.

"Okay, Helen. Now, look. *I* work at Perry and Crowe part time during the school year, full time in the summer. Believe me, I know about this junkie, Atlas. He tried to rob the store this summer."

"I know that," said Helen. "The police told me."

"What else did the cops tell you?"

"Not much except he threw those rocks to get revenge against Mr. Perry, who fired him."

"That's right. Now, first of all, Mr. Perry is a very tough old bird. If we attack him, he will take his ads out of the *Whaler* and see to it that a lot of other town businesses do too. But that's not the point. The point is, if you start writing about this maniac, this doped-up wacko, Atlas, the wrong people might see it, and they might think you know more than you actually do, and they might come after you. Did you ever consider that? Somebody might say, Hey! What did this girl see? What does she know? Stubby and his pals and his old man's pals play very rough. Just please don't get yourself into this. I *knew* Stubby. He worked down in the loading garage. The guy is a hopeless criminal."

"I went to school with him at St. Theresa's. Sort of,"

said Helen. "When I was in second grade, some boy was torturing the class guinea pig. Stubby saved the guinea pig. I remember that."

"And what did he do to the boy?" asked Barry. "Break his arm?"

Helen swallowed hard. "Almost," she admitted. "But—"

"Ellen," said Barry.

"Helen," said Helen.

"Sorry. You ever see *The Godfather*?"

"Yes."

"You want people like that even knowing you exist? I saw plenty of Stubby's friends this summer. They used to wait across the street for him to get off from work. One of them had greasy hair down to his butt. Filthy T-shirt cut off around the middle. He wore a bone twisted in his hair. A bone! Said it was human, but it wasn't. He had a little knife this long, and he could get it out of his pocket in about a fiftieth of a second."

"I get your point," said Helen.

"Good," said Barry.

The *Whaler* office was buzzing frenetically. One of the members of the football team came in and clowned around with Penny Parker. He knocked a bottle of soda on the floor, and someone yelled, "Heads up!"

Beverly took Helen down to the drafting room. She snapped her gum loudly at each step. "Rejection is never easy," said Beverly.

Helen had gotten Barry's point all right. It was just like the nuclear waste trucks. Barry and Jerry and Beverly wouldn't give two hoots if one of the trucks smashed up and contaminated four million people so long as it didn't hurt them or their precious *Whaler*. Jerry and Barry didn't want her to write her story because it might lose them some advertising money. If she got hurt, as Barry so seriously tried to convince her was likely, the only thing he and Jerry would care about was that she might be traced to the *Whaler* and they might not get their stupid award.

As they went into the drafting room, Helen sank the heels of her palms deeply into her eyes, pushing back any tears that might have crept out.

Beverly opened a small bottle of typewriter correcting fluid. "This'll only take a minute," she said, very much like a nurse. Helen handed her the five football player drawings. Beverly held the miniscule brush between two perfectly manicured and pink-polished fingernails. With one neat swipe each of opaque white paint, the faces on Helen's drawings disappeared. "Sign them," said Beverly. "Here's a Rapidograph."

"Sign them?" asked Helen, looking at her precious faceless drawings miserably.

"Sure. I'll just draw in the faces when the photostats come back. You'll get to have your signature on all our new booster tags. Won't that be nice?"

Because tears had welled up in her eyes and she couldn't say a word in argument and didn't dare cry, Helen scrawled her name on the bottom of each drawing. Unreadably.

Beverly looked. "Oh, you can sign better than that!" she said encouragingly and whited out all the signatures.

"Now, sign it nice and clear and legible so everybody can read it and know it's your drawing!" Beverly looked at Helen as if Helen had turned into a real live human-size caterpillar.

"Heaven's sakes!" she exclaimed. "Don't *cry*! Professionals don't cry. Here. I'll sign them for you." Very neatly Beverly wrote *Helen Curry* under each picture. "Pinky!" she yelled into the pressroom at the back. "Get stats of these, will you?"

Beverly took her mirror from her purse. She applied some coral-mist lipstick, which matched her nails, and sauntered up the stairway. As quickly as she was gone, Pinky emerged from the pressroom muttering his usual blasphemy.

"Don't you dare laugh at me, Pinky Levy," Helen sniffed, wiping her eyes with a Kleenex, "or compare me to your awful sister just because I have human feelings!"

"I wasn't going to," said Pinky in complete amazement. "Beverly Boone's the biggest airhead who ever wiggled her fat behind. But crying won't do any good."

"I can't help it," said Helen. "She's a senior, and she's beautiful. I can't say boo to her." Trying hard not to, Helen broke into fresh tears. "That know-it-all Jerry Rosen made her change my drawings. He said I can't write my story because the *Whaler* will lose advertising money. That's all they worry about. And that jerk Barry de Wolf turned down my Hummel drawings again, and he went on like a priest about how somebody out of *The Godfather* might pull a switchblade on me if I wrote the story. All he's trying to do is not embarrass Mr. Perry, his boss, and all he cares about is what the New Bedford businessmen think. He wouldn't bat an eye if somebody strangled me so long as it didn't affect the advertising money for his silly, boring, hideous *Whaler*!"

"Helen," said Pinky.

"Caterpillars," said Helen. "That's what they want. Caterpillars and in-depth studies of birds and . . . and look at this . . . the lead editorial this week about littering in the school parking lot."

"So quit," said Pinky. "If you hate it, quit."

"*No,*" said Helen. She didn't quite know why. The only reason she could think of was that she liked being with Pinky in the pressroom every day, but she certainly wasn't going to say *that*. She wondered if Sister Ignatius had been right. By Monday you'll think you're in love with him, she had observed.

"Sister Ignatius, at the convent, said something interesting," said Helen after a moment.

"A nun?" asked Pinky.

"Don't you dare criticize Catholics," Helen growled at him. "She had a very interesting thing to say about the tip-off note. I showed it to her."

"What?" asked Pinky.

Helen took the folded Xerox copy from her pocketbook and flattened it out under the drafting light. "See this?" Helen pointed with a pencil. "If you just read it through, it looks as if some awful mush-brained idiot wrote it. Spelling, grammar, everything's just terrible. But look at the punctuation. It's perfect. No idiot wrote that note, Pinky. Somebody very well educated, trying to disguise himself as an idiot, wrote it, but he forgot to mess up his punctuation marks."

Pinky stared at the note. He didn't speak for a minute. "Never was any good in English," he said at last, "but I see what you mean. Funny. I took the note over to my Uncle Max. He's a printer. Lives over in Dartmouth. I was curious about the typeface. He said he'd never seen anything like it but couldn't tell what it was without seeing the original."

Pinky drummed his fingers on the drafting table. Helen stared at the inky nails. She felt suddenly as if all the air had been sucked out of the room.

"Are you thinking what I'm thinking?" Pinky asked, folding up the note.

"You mean—"

"The guy in the woods. The one you chased. It *wasn't* Stubby. They got Stubby for throwing the rocks, and he *did* throw them, but the other guy, he was *watching* Stubby. He tipped off the cops. All he wanted was Stubby out of the way. He didn't give a hoot if the lady or the kid died. He just walked away whistling, and then he dropped this note in the squad car and the cops picked up Stubby right away. You know," Pinky went on, "Barry's right. You shouldn't write that story."

"Oh, everybody's always warning me," said Helen. "Barry sounds just like the cops and Sister Ignatius and Aunt Stella."

"Look," said Pinky, "I know Barry's a big windbag. But you should listen to him. He's right. He's a real girl scout, and he advertises his College Board scores all over the school, and he washes his dumb Buick every two days, but he's right. Whoever was in the woods that day might not like to think you're curious about him. He might get scared. And then he might decide to scare you!"

"Pinky," said Helen, "call him a cub scout but not a girl scout. That's a male chauvinist pig remark."

"I don't understand," said Pinky.

"And you never will," said Helen.

It took Pinky most of an hour to clean up his press, but he let Helen help him without once warning her not to get her fingers caught in the rollers.

As Pinky let Helen off his motorbike at the very end of Prospect Avenue, Helen, who had been trying to think of a good insult all the way home, said, "Men have been responsible for all the wars in history. If women ruled the world, there'd be peace."

"Yeah?" said Pinky. "What about What's-her-name in England? And that Dragon Lady in India? And the one from Israel who died? With the frizzy hair."

"You leave Golda Meir's hair alone!" said Helen. She waved to Pinky, who sped off. Walking the rest of the way to the house, she mulled over this brand-new idea. It had never occurred to her that in the history of the world anyone with frizzy hair had ever done anything successful.

She decided that afternoon she would write a letter to Jenny Calhoun, who also suffered from frizzy hair but had a sympathetic mother who styled it nicely. She would tell Jenny this amazing fact about Golda Meir. It meant there was hope for both of them.

"Hi, Aunt Stella!" Helen yelled, dropping her books on the hall table.

No answer.

"Aunt Stella? Aunt Stella, what's wrong?" Aunt Stella was sitting on the button-plush settee. Her teacup rattled in her saucer as she put it down.

"What *is* it, Aunt Stella?"

Aunt Stella indicated something on the coffee table between a toby jug and a bisque ballerina. "I've called your father, and he's coming home right away," said Aunt Stella. "What is the meaning of this, Helen?"

On the table was an ordinary gray plastic tape cassette. Strung through one of the spool holes was a piece of twine, and strung on that was her silver locket.

"Go ahead, open the locket," said Aunt Stella.

Helen opened it. Inside was the photograph of her mother all right, but the eyes had been pierced out with a needle. The eye sockets were bloodred. Her mother's smile was ghostly, grotesque. Helen closed the locket immediately. She felt very unsteady.

"Play the tape," instructed Aunt Stella.

"Did you play it yet?" asked Helen.

"Well, of course I did. The minute I saw that envelope lying under the mail slot."

Helen picked up the envelope. Only her name was on it. She ran her finger over the letters. They were slightly raised, like printing on a wedding invitation.

"It makes no sense at all," said Aunt Stella. "The only thing on the tape is part of a Christmas song."

Helen slid the cassette onto the spools of her tape recorder. There was a short period during which only the steady hum of the tape going around could be heard. Then very clearly the whistling began. This time there was nothing light or musical about it. Each note was perfectly clipped as if he wanted her to sing along, which it was impossible not to do, since the words came into her head as surely as the order of the alphabet. The whistling was low and certain and slow, as if to make sure she would understand:

> *He sees you when you're sleeping,*
> *He knows when you're awake,*
> *He knows if you've been bad or good,*
> *So be good for goodness sake.*
> *Oh! you better watch out . . .*

After only five lines, the whistling stopped and there was only a dead hum on the tape.

Long after her father had come home, gone to the police station with the tape, locket, and envelope, and come back home again, Helen sat in his lap, the side of her face resting on his softly breathing chest, her arms clasped around his back, under his arms. The back of his shirt was damp. It was a hot night. There was nothing left to say. He had answered all her questions, with slight variations, but generally the same way each time. It was a school prank. Things like this happened every day of the week, according to Chief Ryser. He had hundreds of threatening notes and phone calls to deal with every year. Almost every one came from some half-crazy coward with a grudge of some kind. Even Ryser's son had gotten a few threatening notes in the mail. It turned out someone in his class thought the boy had ratted on him for cheating on a math test.

"Dad, the eyes! Mother's eyes were bloody red!"

"And I told you before, there was just a bit of red backing paper behind the photograph. That's all."

"But, Dad, before there was no red backing paper. I swear! The photograph popped out of the locket last summer—the summer before anyway. There was no backing paper of any kind. Beside that, if it was just a piece of paper behind the photograph, why didn't the pin or needle—or whatever he used to poke her eyes out—why didn't that pierce *both* pieces of paper at the same time? Why? Why did he leave just the eye sockets looking bloody red and not make holes in the backing paper? Why?"

"How can anyone figure out a thing like that?" her father said. "Now everything's going to be all right."

He went on to tell her what a hectic, nuisance-filled evening poor Chief Ryser was having. While they'd been talking in the police station parking lot, all kinds of minor disasters had been reported within her father's earshot over Ryser's CB radio. Helen knew how it had gone—with the two men, probably rocking back and forth on their heels, hands in pockets, assuring each other that this was just kid's stuff. Ryser probably talked about football. Most men did. And her dear father probably mentioned a few local toxic waste dumps in passing. That or what he always called "the lost tribe of Israel," his beloved, stumbling Boston Red Sox.

Helen removed her arms from around him.

"Feeling better?" he asked.

She looked up at him. With his smile, his sea-blue eyes, and his lovely head of hair, he receded from her like a comet heading for a remote star, although his arms, strong and warm, held her close.

"Yes, I feel okay, Dad," said Helen. This was a lie.

After supper Aunt Stella left for her weekly bridge game with many warnings about locking windows and doors. Taking a whistle out of her purse, she told Helen to blow it as hard as she could into the receiver should an obscene phone caller ring up, in order at least to get him in the eardrum.

As the house was stuffy, Helen's father opened all the windows and doors the minute Aunt Stella's car pulled out of the driveway. The Red Sox and Yankees were playing in a critical series. When the television went on, Helen was able to call Pinky without being overheard. Pinky promised to be at her house in ten minutes. He told her to have the envelope ready for him.

"What are you going to do with it?" Helen asked.

"Take it to my Uncle Max, the printer. All he said he needed was an original."

"Pinky," said Helen, "you know what this means?"

"What?"

"It means we're . . . we're getting into this deeper. If we trace his printing press through your Uncle Max, it means we're following him."

"He's following you, isn't he?" asked Pinky abruptly and hung up.

Helen tried to take some pleasure in the thought that Pinky cared and wanted to protect her, but she could not. She went down to the kitchen and got two bottles of Coke from the icebox and, quietly opening the front door, over the chatter of the television in the den, she placed them in the milk-bottle box. She was not going to lie. She was not going to sneak out of the house, and she was not, for one minute, going to miss Uncle Max.

"Dad, please," she asked again and again, "just for a soda."

"No!" said her father as many times, not taking his gaze off the baseball players. "Silver dollars on my eyes before I let you leave this house."

Helen waited. Twenty-five minutes passed before Pinky came. She let him in without a word, her finger pressed to her lips.

"Hello, sir," said Pinky in his best West Point cadet voice.

Helen's father gave him a dark look with a kernel of humor in back of it. "Trying to butter me up like a piece of toast?" he asked, suppressing the twinkle in his eyes.

For fifteen minutes Pinky and Helen's father shouted and groaned over the game in progress. After the Red Sox had scored three runs, Pinky asked if it would be all right to take Helen out for a soda.

"You know about the locket and everything?" asked her father, reaching deep into a cracker box.

"Yes, sir, but please don't worry."

Her father brushed some cracker crumbs off his lap onto the rug. "You *are* Sam Levy's son, aren't you?" he asked.

"Yes, well, he was my father until he died." Helen could feel Pinky's mind zooming around. "I mean, he's still my father. Yes."

Helen's father smiled. "Sam was a good man," he said. "Wish I'd had time to know him better. You can go. But

I'm warning you. Be back before Stella at ten-forty-five, or she'll put all three of our heads in the food processor."

Pinky straddled his motorbike, balancing on the seat while he examined the envelope and the locket and played the tape three times over on the recorder.

Helen sat on the ground beside the motorcycle. When Pinky took off the earphones, she asked, "Does it scare you?"

"It scares me," said Pinky. "God, that song . . . I always hated that song when I was a little tiny kid. I used to lie in bed even in July and think about being watched all the way from the North Pole. It never bothered me that God was looking straight down from heaven and seeing everything. What bothered me was thinking Santa Claus had eyesight that followed the curve of the earth and . . . You look pale."

Helen tried to rub some color into her cheeks. She opened both Cokes and tried to get the words to the song out of her head. They would not go. "I don't understand," she said at last. "I *didn't* write that article."

"Whoever it is thinks you know too much, all the same," said Pinky. "Your name was in the paper with your address. Maybe he saw you in the woods. You've been talking about writing this article to just about everybody. Someone you talked to could have told someone else. The word got out anyway. Maybe you ought to go home. Let me go to Uncle Max. Nobody's after *me*."

"Yet," said Helen.

"Yet," Pinky agreed.

Helen took the locket back from Pinky. Her father had promised he would find another nice picture of her mother for it. Well, she didn't want another nice picture. He had poked out her mother's eyes, and maybe he had it in mind to poke out hers. He would wait for her, in her imagination, now, in the shadow of every tree and wall. He would sit unseen at movie theaters, stand hidden on streets, watching her. He would follow her home and stare at her, faceless, through the windows of her house while she ate and slept.

"Like hell I'll go home, Pinky," she said.

The bumpy, mosquito-ridden trip to Dartmouth dragged like a bad year. Uncle Max made it worthwhile.

"Max Levy," he said, extending an ink-stained hand to Helen and pumping hers happily. He explained that he was Pinky's only relative who was not blond and good-looking. Uncle Max's hair was almost gone, his glasses smudged, and his smile as beatific as a child's.

His basement workshop ran the whole length and breadth of his house and was filled with small presses, parts of presses, complete and incomplete fonts made of metal and wood, parts of typewriters, and stacks of books. He showed Helen his collection of hundred-year-old wooden type fonts, rescued, he said, from a warehouse about to be torn down in Taunton. He spoke of them as if they'd been children rescued from a fire.

Uncle Max made them each a glass of ice tea with fresh mint leaves and poured himself a crystal goblet of Riesling from a half bottle he kept in a small under-the-counter refrigerator. Then he switched on a brilliant light over his work table, pulled on a pair of surgeon's gloves, and examined the envelope and the copy of the tip-off note. He looked at them this way and that and then placed them under a giant desk magnifier that was bolted to the edge of the table. Several times he ran his fingers over the type on the envelope, and once he measured the lines with a ruler marked not in inches but in some other measurement Helen did not know. He murmured little bits of things to himself and hummed, the whole time, parts of the national anthem. "Too bad this is all you've got," he said. "Still . . ."

He put the envelope and the note down and began consulting his books. He went from one to the next, frowning and looking in indexes and going back over the same pages again and again. "Funny," he said more to himself than to Pinky and Helen. "Impossible really. But then . . . If this came from the Smithsonian in Washington, I wouldn't have any trouble at all. I just find it hard to believe."

"What, Uncle Max?" asked Pinky, breaking his impatient silence. "What is it?"

"It's a Thurber," said Uncle Max. "No question. Look here." He positioned the magnifier so that Pinky and Helen could both see through it. He pointed with a pair of tweezers. "Do you see that every character, that means letter," he added for Helen's benefit, "every character has a tiny little ridge or line underneath it? See that?"   ◄

"I see it," said Pinky. "It isn't inked, but it's there. It shows up like a shadow on the Xerox copy."

"Okay," said Uncle Max. He folded his glasses and put them in his shirt pocket. "When you set type, what's the first thing you do before you ink and print?"

"You lock it in, of course," said Pinky.

"Right," said Uncle Max, and for Helen's understanding he explained again, making a little drawing as he did. "See?" he said. "When you set a line of type, each piece, each letter, is attached to a heavy block, metal or wood. You make a line with your words, and then you slip a bar over the top and under the bottom of the line. It's called locking it in. That keeps everything straight, and the pieces of type don't slide around. Now, these little ridges on your envelope and note here are uneven. If this envelope, say, had been done on a printing press, it would have been locked in and the little ridges would be even, but they aren't even." Uncle Max looked at Pinky. "You said on the telephone the police think it was done on a cheap toy set?"

Pinky nodded.

"Even a cheap rubber toy set has to be locked in or you can't print," said Uncle Max.

"What does that mean?" asked Helen.

"It means both the note and the envelope were written on an extremely old typewriter, or writing machine, as it was called in those days. Before the Civil War. Now, most people think the typewriter was invented around 1880, which is true actually. At least it came into commercial use then. But way back in about 1847 there was a man called Burt and another called Thurber. They fooled around with this writing machine idea. Your note and envelope were typed on a Thurber machine made over in Worcester in 1847. Both samples match the one in my book exactly. Take a look. What confirms it is the raised lettering. You see, Mr. Thurber meant his machine as a sort of braille writer too, so that blind people could read the type with their fingertips. He never got anywhere with it. It was a dismal failure. He spent the rest of his life manufacturing sextants and compasses for ships."

Helen and Pinky looked at the sample in Uncle Max's book. "It matches exactly," said Helen. "Every letter is the same."

"It's very strange," said Uncle Max. "There are only two Thurbers known to exist in the world. One's in the Smithsonian in Washington, and the other's in a typewriter museum in England. A Thurber is a very rare beetle indeed. There must have been another one. No wonder your cops, with all the best intentions, couldn't find it."

The envelope and the tip-off note rested bleakly on the table beneath the dazzling work light. A photograph of the Smithsonian Institution's Thurber was reproduced next to the sample. It looked more like an unsuccessful musical instrument than an unsuccessful typewriter. Helen read through the sample in the book. It was an incomplete letter to President Polk, dated March 8, 1848, announcing the invention of the machine itself.

Somewhere in the back of Helen's mind the horrible little Christmas song began to play again. "He knows if you've been bad or good, so be good for goodness sake." The locket was in her shirt-front pocket, the picture, eyeless. How would he do it to her if *she* wasn't good. Would he hold her down? She would fight and scream like a tiger. Somehow he'd probably knock her out first. Then it would be easy to get at her eyes.

Miles in the distance thunder volleyed and boomed from the south, as if awakening some long-dead secret by force.

Uncle Max sat in a tattered Barcalounger and poured himself the last inch of Riesling in the bottle. Cleaning the smudges off his glasses, he asked gently, "I wonder who could have a Thurber?"

SEVEN

Helen watched Mr. Brzostoski's eyes. He had switched the tape to the beginning again and was listening intently. She worried that although he had no foreign accent whatever, he might have been born in Europe and the words to the song would not come easily to him as they had to her and to Pinky.

When he'd heard it through once more, he took the orange sponge earphones off his head and asked, "*Who* did the police tell your father it was?"

"Some old singer called Bing Crosby who used to whistle on the radio," said Helen. "Ryser thought it was 'White Christmas,' which it isn't."

"Did your father point that out? Did he show Ryser the envelope?"

"He said it was done on a toy set."

"Voiceprints? Fingerprints?"

"Can't voiceprint whistling. Aunt Stella, me, my father had all handled the cassette. Mr. Bro, I told you they thought it was a joke."

"And you think I will look at this differently?"

"Well . . . do you?" Helen asked.

"I don't know. I'll have to think about it."

"At least," said Helen, "will you help me, Mr. Bro? You're a history teacher. Will you tell me how to go about looking for a hundred-and-forty-year-old writing machine?"

"Not if it's in the hands of some maniac, I won't."

"Then you *do* believe me?" Helen asked, unable to keep either the sharpness or the honey out of her voice.

Mr. Bro did not answer until he had finished an entire banana. He folded the skin neatly on his blotter. "Yes," he said, just as neatly. "But I can't help you."

Helen stood. "Then I'll do it myself," she said. "I'll find a way."

"Sit down. No, you won't," said Mr. Bro. "Helen, I'm a teacher. A responsible adult. I can't let you go off the deep end looking for an old typewriter with some nut who uses it. Some nut who pokes out eyes."

"You think that's what he means to do to me?"

"Of *course* that's what he means to do. He's telling you, you better be good and you better watch out. He has quite deliberately punched out the eyes in the photograph, then placed red paper, cut out exactly in the shape of the locket, behind the picture to give the impression of . . . forgive me, gouged out eyes. If this had been simple backing paper, both papers would have holes in them. Beside that . . ." Mr. Bro removed the photo of Helen's mother carefully and set it on the desk. He took out the red paper behind it, touched his finger to his tongue, and rubbed it across the tiny scarlet scrap. "Ink," he declared, looking at his reddened thumb. "Ink. Somebody's gone to the trouble of coloring that bit of paper with red ink. If it were backing paper or anything else manufactured or printed, it wouldn't come off with a lick of my finger, would it? So. That's a warning. It's clear as day."

"If it's so clear to you and me and to Pinky, how come they won't listen? Why, Mr. Bro?"

Mr. Bro smiled a little bitterly. He folded up the copy of the tip-off note and placed it with the locket and the cassette in the envelope. "If he—whoever it is—cut out letters, say from the newspaper, and pasted them on a sheet of stationery and directly said, 'Keep out of this or I'll poke your eyes out,' believe me the cops would have sat up and taken notice. He's clever, this fellow. He did it in just such a way as to scare the living daylights out of you and make the cops laugh."

"What—" Helen began.

"Just let me think," said Mr. Bro. He swiveled in his chair and gazed out the window, murmuring tiny sounds. Then he swiveled back and faced her. "What would happen," he asked, "if you went back to the police and showed them Uncle Max's book and proved to them that both the tip-off note about Stubby's rock throwing and the threat to you, the envelope anyway, were typed on an identical machine and that it wasn't a toy at all? It's a rare antique."

"I think the cops have kind of had it with me," said Helen. "They think *I'm* a nut."

"Okay. You're right. It was just a thought. I can go to the police *for* you, of course. But I need more than this. There's a sergeant on the force, name's Sandy Reynolds. I tutored his son for free last year. He owes me a favor. But first we have to have the location of that machine. That— what is it?—Thurber. And before we even think of doing that, I have to know you're safe."

"Safe?"

"Safe," repeated Mr. Bro. "Let's see what we know. We know this guy has an education. He knows how to punctuate beautifully. He whistles, but not just tootleydo. He whistles like James Galway. You know who James Galway is?"

"Of course," said Helen. "Irish flutist. Dad took me to his concert in Boston last April."

"Good for you," said Mr. Bro. "And you know he uses a typewriter so old and so unusual there are only two others known in the world. Was there a picture of this Thurber in Uncle Max's book?"

"Yes. It looked more like a funny old . . . well, sort of like a funny old harpsichord or carpenter's machine. It's big. About as high as this desk. And it has lots of wooden knobs and rollers—"

"Rickety? Delicate?"

"I think so."

"Then it probably hasn't been moved. It's likely it's still in its original location because it's in working order," said Mr. Bro, "and moving it would almost certainly have broken it. Now, you say the tip-off note was put in the squad car around six o'clock? On the corner of Wharf and Broad?"

"Yes."

"And he was up in the woods an hour before. He'd have to get out of the woods . . . somehow get down to Wharf Street in about forty-five minutes. Not much time. My guess is the machine is in New Bedford. Not far. The bad thing is the town is full of old warehouses, attics, houses, you name it. The good thing is he doesn't know you saw the tip-off note in the police station, or that Pinky made a copy of it, or that you went to Uncle Max and traced it to the Thurber. So, very quietly, you must find this machine. If you do it exactly the way I tell you, he'll never guess what you're up to, even if he is watching you from time to time. He'll be happy, because you'll be good, just as he wants. Then, when you find where it is, I promise to go to Sergeant Reynolds." Mr. Bro looked straight up for a second, smiled, and wrote something on a piece of paper. "Here," he said. "Your official assignment is History of the Writing Machine, Civil War Era. I will assign similar papers to the rest of the class, which they will hate. Threshing machines, sewing machines, reaping machines. You will keep me informed every single step of the way. Eat this Hershey bar and pray that whoever is after you won't find out what you're up to while I explain how you should start."

Helen munched on the chocolate. While she listened to Mr. Bro, Sister Ignatius's explanation of the power of prayer came suddenly into her mind and stuck there. It was as crisply imprinted in her memory as the word *Hershey* was on the candy wrapper.

Sister Ignatius despised the religion textbook as much as Mr. Bro despised the history textbook. She taught her students that the power of good was greater than the power of evil. "However, dear children," she added to this, "do not for one minute think the good Lord is a public official who rushes around answering every prayer like a mayor answering ten phones at once. Do not suppose that in His great wisdom He reaches down into our world like a herring fisherman with a net to pluck every fallen child from the road or every sparrow from the mouth of a fox."

Mr. Oliver Jenkins, curator of the New Bedford Preservation Society, was an apologetic young man with wispy hair and pink-rimmed eyes. He showed Helen the bank of files. "We're going to have them microfilmed in a couple of weeks," he said mournfully, "but until then . . ."

There were four thousand eight hundred and ninety folders, each one so dusty that on Thursday, the third day of her search, Helen brought with her a whole box of Kleenex and a Vicks inhaler. Her eye rims had taken on the same pinkish tinge that Oliver Jenkins's had, and Aunt Stella had said she was going to take her to the doctor for her mysterious allergies. On Friday Helen brought Pinky along. He said he hated papers, city halls, and preservation societies, but Helen convinced him he didn't have to read anything. He just had to find a paper or document with typing on it from the years 1847 to 1880.

"Why 1880?" Pinky asked.

"Because that's when commercial typewriters were invented. A Thurber would have been outdated by then."

Pinky sat in an unforgiving oak chair under an excruciatingly dim ceiling light with file number 3020. Helen took up file number 3050, and Oliver Jenkins, in another uncomfortable oak chair, sat with them and made notes on old railroad maps and chewed to bits the stem of an unlit corncob pipe.

Friday afternoon at four-thirty they finished.

"I knew you wouldn't find anything," said Oliver Jenkins when Helen replaced the last file in the last drawer. "Sorry we couldn't help you," he went on. "But everybody knows there were no typewriters until about 1885. Even then it was considered bad manners to type." He folded his railway map with care. "After the First World War, of course, everybody typed. But then, you're not interested in the First World War."

"No," said Helen as kindly as she could. She sneezed. Pinky took a sniff of the Vicks. "There *was* such a machine, though, and it was here in New Bedford," she added hopefully, but feeling no hope at all.

"All those files," said Oliver Jenkins mournfully. "It's not in them, is it?"

"No," said Helen, thinking what a good undertaker Oliver Jenkins would have been and hoping desperately he would have some other files or ideas.

He went on grudgingly. "Of course I only believe in hard, factual research, but I hate to see you get a failing grade on your history paper, so I might as well suggest you go see Asa Roche."

Helen's eyes lit up. Pinky asked, "Who?"

"He's a very old man, very old," said Oliver Jenkins, as

if he expected Asa Roche to be dead in the morning. "There aren't many of the old people left who might still remember. He must have been born around 1890 or so. He won't remember the Civil War days of course, but the Thurber machine would have been an unusual invention back then. Perhaps his parents or his grandparents re-marked on it to him. Doubtful though." Oliver Jenkins took one of Helen's Kleenexes and blew his nose. "He or his sister, Elizabeth Fairchild, might be able to tell you who had the first telephone in New Bedford or the first electric lights. You might as well try, even though you'll probably fail. You'll have a hard time getting in the front door. Elizabeth Fairchild guards the house like a mastiff."

"Can't you comb your hair just a little?" asked Helen.

"I don't carry a comb," said Pinky. "What do think I am? A greaser?"

The old and dignified streets of colonial New Bedford sailed past the windows of the bus. Helen kept her eyes sharp, looking for 156 Orchard Street. "Besides that," Pinky grumbled, "you're the one with the hair around here. Not me."

Helen hated to think that Pinky noticed her hair. Today was a very frizzy day due to the humidity. She glanced at her well-shined shoes and then at Pinky's sneakers, which were worn and filthy and had two differ-ent color laces. "It's just that it's going to be hard enough getting through Elizabeth Fairchild without giving her more to object to," said Helen.

"What exactly do you mean by 'more to object to'?" Pinky asked.

Helen checked the house numbers. They were now passing the high three hundreds.

"Old Elizabeth might go in for shoeshines and neckties," she said.

"Neckties!" Pinky squealed.

"Shush!" said Helen. "We're on a crowded bus. In the historic district!"

"I *won't* shush," said Pinky. "You're worse than most females. Boy! You'll give a man a hard time someday, Miss Brillo-head!"

"Don't you ever call me that again, Pinky Levy!" she snapped, biting off the end of every word.

"I'll say what I like."

"You apologize for that."

"I'm staying on the bus," said Pinky loftily. "You can go see them yourself, Miss Shiny Shoes."

Helen stood up and grabbed hold of a strap. As she did, she heard a familiar voice.

"Ellen! There you are. What are you doing here? I haven't seen you down at the *Whaler* in a week!"

Helen ground her teeth. Filled with guilt, she faced Barry, who'd been sitting behind them all the time listening to every word of their conversation and hearing Pinky call her Miss Brillo-head. "I'm researching a history paper for Mr. Bro," she said weakly.

"Where are the Hummel drawings?" asked Barry.

"Not finished," said Helen. "I've been working on them all week."

"When do you expect to finish them?" Barry asked.

"Very soon!" said Helen. She hadn't looked at them for days. Worst of all Aunt Stella had not been able to replace the chipped Hummel figurine yet. There were no more like it at Perry and Crowe. Aunt Stella had promised to drive to a store in Fall River to buy one.

"All right," said Barry. "But don't forget. Bring the figurine back when you finish the drawings." Barry collected his books and swung himself down the steps of the bus. "Don't forget!" he called out to her again. The bus lurched onward.

Pinky was grinning at her. "Aunt Stella get a new statue for you yet?" he asked.

"You know perfectly well she didn't, Pinky Levy. I told you."

"Come on," said Pinky. "We've got better things to do than worry about that. This looks like the right stop."

Helen banged the brass door knocker at the Fairchild house loudly but an eternity seemed to pass before the door was answered. Then Elizabeth Fairchild, her hair in a shining silver wave, was looking down at them with cold lapis lazuli eyes over a nose like a hatchet. She measured Pinky and Helen with some internal yardstick and asked them why it was they wanted to speak to Mr. Roche.

"It's for a school assignment," Helen answered brightly, dredging up the safe and familiar reason. Adults never argued with school assignments for fear of obstructing education. "New Bedford history," Helen added.

"Mr. Roche is resting. He is not well," said Mrs. Fairchild in a final sort of voice. She obviously did not care a fig for education.

"Lizzy!" yelled a scratchy voice from somewhere inside the house. "Lizzy? Who is it?"

Mrs. Fairchild turned. "It's no one, Asa!" she shouted

back. Then she stared severely at Helen's plaintive face and at Pinky's sneaker laces. "A few minutes only, then," she said. "He tires easily."

Mrs. Fairchild led them to an upstairs sitting room. Asa Roche looked extremely well to Pinky and Helen.

"Let's have some tea, Lizzy," he suggested when they had sat down on a hard sofa and Mrs. Fairchild had placed herself near the doorway like a sentinel. Reluctantly she agreed to tea.

"That'll take her some time," cackled Asa Roche with a grin. "Minute I heard the door knocker, I hid the tea." He ambled over to the mantelpiece and removed one of the two Staffordshire spaniels that sat on either side of a Staffordshire clock. He smiled at the sound of distant cupboards being opened and slammed shut in the search for tea. He screwed off the head of the spaniel, drank deeply from it, and put it back. "I like young people," he said with a contented sigh. Then he added, "The doctor keeps my bottle filled for me. It's just vodka. She can't smell it. The reason she's such a crotchety old hoddy-doddy is she thinks I'm going to cut her out of my will," said Asa with another impossible cackle.

"Asa!" Mrs. Fairchild's angry voice floated upstairs from the kitchen. "Asa! Where did you put the tea?"

"In with the ice cubes, dear," Asa Roche bellowed back. In his softly crinkled pink face was the wickedness of a puppy who had swallowed a stick of butter. "Lizzy's got a surprise coming when I snuff out," he went on. "I didn't make a will."

"Oh?" asked Helen politely.

"Nope! Nope! No will at all. Course she'll get my

money all the same from the state of Massachusetts since she's my only living relative. I don't want the old fossil to starve. All her husband's family have died out. On the other hand, I do want the last laugh, that's all. For years she's been feeding me boiled beef and carrots with a puddle of water in the plate and depriving me of my one comfort." He looked at the trick bottle on the mantel. "Now, what can I do for you folks?"

Helen glanced at Pinky and then back at Mr. Roche. "We came just on the chance that you might remember something from long, long ago," she explained. "It goes back to Civil War times. A typewriter, or a writing machine, as it was called back then. It was made over in Worcester by a man named Thurber."

"I'm not *that* old," said Asa Roche.

"Oh, I'm sorry, Mr. Roche. I didn't mean that. I just thought maybe your parents or grandparents might have told you about it."

Asa Roche yanked on his earlobe and shook his head. "Nope," he said. "Can't say I ever heard of such a thing."

Despite herself, Helen began to cry. It was hopeless.

Asa Roche frowned at her in alarm. "I'm so sorry I can't help you," he said. "Here, let me get you a handkerchief."

"It's all right," said Helen. "It was just I was so hoping that . . ."

"I heard you tell Lizzy it was for a school paper. It must be a pretty important school paper to get you crying. Here!" he said kindly. "I'll show you another trick. Look at this." Asa Roche shuffled over to a desk that stood in the corner. It was an enormous mahogany secretary. The feet were gigantic lions' paws, and snaking vines with bunches of grapes ran up the sides and inexplicably turned into lions' heads at all four top corners. The lions' mouths were open, lips curled in fearful wooden snarls. Beneath shaggy wooden brows the lions' eyes were green glass.

Asa Roche pushed the left eye of the left rear lion. Immediately a whirring and popping sound began, and out of the lion's head rose a small wooden box, beautifully shaped with a tiny brass door in it.

Pinky was entranced. Asa grinned at him. "The desk belonged to an old geezer called Lorenzo Fairchild," he explained. He opened the little door. Out spilled about thirty buttons. He picked them up and put them back. Then he turned to Helen, who did not look a bit cheered up by the desk with the secret compartment. "Take one," he said and handed a button to Helen. "It's solid gold," he added. "Don't tell Lizzy, though. She'll put me on bread and water for two weeks!"

"Thank you, Mr. Roche," said Helen. She slipped the button into her purse. Asa Roche was so kind. At least she would have something to string on the empty chain that had held her locket.

"Yup," Asa went on. "Solid gold. Came off old Lorenzo's uniform. See him up there?" He pointed to a dark photograph of a portly, middle-aged man in a Civil War uniform. "Lorenzo was friends with Lincoln himself," Asa went on. "Grandfather of my sister Lizzy's husband, John Fairchild. Lincoln made him a general. If you ask me, he didn't deserve it. He never spent a day in danger. If you ask me, he was a war profiteer. That's all."

"What's that?" asked Pinky.

Asa Roche's face was wreathed in smiles. "Lorenzo Fairchild found more ways to make money than six Rockefellers," he answered. "Nobody like him before or since. Made a mint importing arms and munitions from Great Britain during the Civil War. He was in whaling first, of course. Then, when they discovered oil in Pennsylvania, why, he went and invented a way to refine Pennsylvania crude oil here in New Bedford before they found out how to do it in Pennsylvania. He was some fellow, believe me. Died many years before my time. Strong as an ox, smart as a whip, mean as a snake. Lorenzo was the first man in town to install indoor plumbing and gas lamps. He even had a private railway line run up to his house. Lorenzo Fairchild was the first man in New Bedford to wear long trousers 'stead of breeches. Did you know that?"

"No," said Helen. "I didn't." Pinky was trying out the secret drawer and all the other lions' eyes to see if anything else happened.

"You know, it's funny," said Asa. "A typewriter would have been a very newfangled item back then, wouldn't it? I'd make a bet that if anybody in this town had a machine like that in those days, it would have been Lorenzo. He had every gadget and contrivance to come along. He or his poor benighted daughter, Lucy. She was just like him in that respect."

"What happened to Lucy?" asked Pinky.

Asa shuffled over to the door and listened. "Thought

she was on her way," he said. "Lucy?" He laughed saucily. "Lucy was her dad's favorite. She was a caution, so they say. A card. Dressed up like a boy. Once she went on one of his whaling ships, and the captain didn't know till they'd rounded Cape Horn that he had a girl on board. My mother told me that story. Lucy threw harpoons with the best of them, she said."

"But what happened to her?" asked Pinky.

There was a tinkling sound from the kitchen. Asa heard it. "Vanished," he said. "Nobody ever knew. She was forgotten. Lorenzo had gotten himself elected mayor of New Bedford by that time. He erased every memory of his own flesh and blood. Every trace of her. There's no record of her anywhere."

"Why?" asked Helen.

Asa Roche shrugged. "Nobody knows," he said. "Lorenzo tried to get the house he'd given her as a wedding present condemned as a public pestilence. Town wouldn't go that far, of course, even if he was mayor, so he got a couple of convicts from the jail to burn it down one night. No one knows where the house—" Here there was a great clanking and squeaking. Mrs. Fairchild entered the room with a silver tea service that looked as if it weighed over seventy pounds. Helen and Pinky jumped up to help her but were stopped by a withering glance, and Mrs. Fairchild placed the heavy tray on the table as if it were as light as tin.

Elizabeth Fairchild had reached out a strong left arm to pour when Helen remarked earnestly, "What a wonderful thing to talk with your brother, Mrs. Fairchild. He was just telling us the story of Lucy Fairchild. She sounds like such a colorful ancestor." The arm holding the teapot stopped in midair and then put it abruptly back on the tray. "Time for your medicine, Asa!" she announced. "Come, children!"

Helen and Pinky found themselves very quickly in the hallway and following Mrs. Fairchild's starchy back down the echoing stairs. Asa could still be heard through the thick door to his room. "I told 'em, Lizzy!" he shrieked. "Dizzy Lizzy, kids! That's what they called her when she was young!"

Helen expected more bile from Elizabeth Fairchild. Instead, in the foyer she addressed them with something closer to throaty kindness in her tone. Piously she clasped her hands in front of her and fluttered her head, as if she were bothered by a fly. "I apologize, children," she said, "for my brother. As you can see, I had good reason not to want you to see him. His mind wanders dreadfully now, and he makes up things out of whole cloth. May I ask the subject of your history paper?"

"Oh, yes," said Helen. "We really only wanted to ask him about a typewriter. A very old one."

"A *typewriter?*" Elizabeth Fairchild sounded both relieved and astonished.

"Yes," said Helen. "Mr. Roche told us that if anybody were to have such a thing back in Civil War times, it would have been Lorenzo Fairchild."

"Well," answered Mrs. Fairchild grudgingly, "he's right there, of course. Lorenzo Fairchild was quite an inventor and an entrepreneur. He made the family fortune with his enterprising ideas."

"Have you ever seen or heard of a typewriter being used back then?" Pinky asked.

Mrs. Fairchild studied the far end of the living room for a moment. She wasn't bothered by this question, at least, Helen decided. Finally she shook her head decisively. "No. I very much doubt it, unless one of his companies had one. Lorenzo wrote a beautiful hand. He kept many diaries. They are all over at the Fairchild mansion down the street if you wish to see them."

Helen cleared her throat.

"Mrs. Fairchild," said Helen, "we must find this typewriter. Some nut, some maniac, is using it and he's threatening me. Mr. Roche said that perhaps Lorenzo's daughter, Lucy—"

But Mrs. Fairchild cut her off, this time with fire in her icy voice. "I thought you said this was for a school paper," she said.

"Well, I did, but the real reason—"

"I don't like people who change their stories in midstream," snapped Mrs. Fairchild. "If somebody is threatening you, go to the police." This settled, her tone turned patronizing.

"My brother, Asa, is a very old man, child. His memory is seriously impaired at times. He puts the tea in the freezer and the ice in the cupboards. He cannot find the daily newspaper when it is lying in his lap." She paused for a sharp breath. "There were four Fairchild sisters," she said, "as Asa well knows—Clara, Constance, Blanche, and Virginia. If you care to go to the Fairchild mansion, you will find all of their papers and a complete collection of family records and photographs. This Lucy is a figment of Asa's imagination." And quite primly and as if Helen had suggested Jesus Christ had a twin sister, she added, "No such person ever existed."

The day had turned cold when Pinky and Helen left the house and began their long walk down Orchard Street to the bus stop. No bus was in sight, but they both hurried to the small, ugly metal-sided shelter on the corner. Helen drew her sweater around herself closely. The shelters were supposed to deflect the winter's blast and the summer's baking sun. In reality, of course, they turned into either wind tunnels or ovens, depending on the season.

The side of the bus shelter was solid sheet metal. The only window was low down, at foot level. "Look at the dumb way they design these things," said Pinky. "Are you supposed to get down on your hands and knees to see if a bus is coming?"

Helen didn't answer. She had glanced through the bottom window of the bus shelter, and now she reached for Pinky's sleeve and pulled him back against her before he could go in. Through the window she had seen a pair of legs, bare and crossed at the ankles. On the side of the left sneaker was the word *Nike* in blue. The *e* was missing.

"What?" Pinky began, but Helen hushed him, trembling, her eyes wide. She discovered she'd dropped her books. She didn't care.

"The shoes . . . the shoes . . . *his* shoes! He's in there!" she whispered.

"Okay," Pinky whispered back. "Let's go in and see—"

"No," said Helen. The policeman's warnings, Sister Ignatius's doubts, and Barry's man with the bone in his hair and quick little knife burned in her mind. She pulled

Pinky behind a huge horse-chestnut tree, leaving her books on the sidewalk.

"Don't talk," Helen whispered. "Just see who gets on the bus." Minute after minute they watched the legs moving, crossing and uncrossing, through the window at a distance of about twenty feet.

At last the bus lumbered down the street. Hidden behind the trees, Helen counted the seconds until it stopped, and the door opened with an asthmatic squeal. Out of the bus shelter crept a large-boned woman, known locally as Dora, her hair flying in her face in the wind. She was dressed entirely in towels, safety-pinned together, and carried two shopping bags crammed with newspapers. The door closed, and the bus left.

Dead leaves scurried along the cobblestones as they did in December. Helen and Pinky picked up Helen's scattered books and papers and, that done, sat in the wind-filled shelter against a graffiti-covered wall. Helen kicked a spiny horse chestnut into the gutter. "Everything . . . everything turns into nothing," she said at last.

"Please," said Pinky. "Don't cry. Don't shake like that."

"I can't help it."

Pinky took off his worn brown cardigan and laid it over Helen's bent shoulders. "We'll find him. Don't worry," he said.

"No, we won't," said Helen. "We'll never, ever find him. Look, he's even thrown his sneakers away in some trash heap for a bag lady to find. We'll never find him."

"Yes, we will. I promise we will."

"Pinky, *how*? We went through every file in the Preservation Society looking for that Thurber. A whole week of dusty papers for nothing. I went through the Fairchild papers under *F* on Wednesday. There was no Thurber there in all their records. Everything was handwritten. I had a little hope back then, when Asa Roche started talking about Lucy. I thought, well, just maybe this will lead somewhere. But old Elizabeth Fairchild took care of that. Lucy was just a figment of Asa's imagination."

The next bus showed as a speck at the end of the street. Pinky picked up Helen's books with his own. He took her hand in his and, holding it tightly, said, "I wouldn't believe old Dizzy Lizzy Fairchild if she told me there was ten cents in a dime."

EIGHT

Saturday morning at eleven o'clock Pinky was kicked out of the Fairchild mansion for dropping a priceless piece of scrimshaw, point down, on the parquet floor. The scrimshaw, being pure ivory, did not break, but the parquet was visibly dented, and so the custodian told Pinky to leave and never come back. Pinky left. He called the custodian a fish-faced old barnacle as he went out the door.

It took until Sunday afternoon for the custodian to get over this and warm up to Helen. In the end, Helen guessed, he was a lonely man. Not many people came to the Fairchild mansion after the summer tourists left. He wore a livery uniform, dark green with gold braid, like a doorman. He knew by heart the regulation spiel about the Fairchild family history that he obviously gave to all visitors. Helen was not interested in the relics of whaling days or the relics of the old Slater Mills. She listened with half an ear to stories of pirates attacking Fairchild ships and Roger Peddie Fairchild, who crossed the Delaware River with George Washington himself.

She was interested only in the Thurber, and through Lorenzo and the Fairchild sisters she hoped to find it.

The custodian had scoffed at the idea of there ever having been such a thing as a Thurber typewriter in the family. And by Sunday at three Helen had concluded he was right. She had gone through all Lorenzo's diaries and fifty-eight boxes of correspondence belonging to his daughters, Virginia, Blanche, Clara, and Constance. Every letter, diary entry, list, every snippet of paper in the place was handwritten. And there was no Lucy. No Lucy anywhere.

Helen was about to go. The custodian took off again on one of his sermons. Helen sat respectfully at a long English-oak table in the middle of the library. The custodian pulled up a chair. He tweaked his military mustache, and his pink cheeks glowed with the happiness of having someone to talk to. "Good manners," Aunt Stella had told Helen many times, "mean being considerate of others' feelings when you yourself are tired, bored, or out of sorts." Helen was all three and terrified. Her father was going to pick her up at the mansion because she thought somebody might follow her down the street, although she hadn't told him this.

She tried to listen to the old man describe what he called the Bedford Ladies' Aide Society. He had given her a large box of Fairchild family photographs and a pair of white cotton gloves to put on so as not to get fingerprints on them. "The earliest ones," he said, "were called daguerreotypes. The others were called tintypes or ambrotypes."

Helen looked through the photographs.

"I suppose you're fascinated by all those lists the Fairchild sisters kept," he said.

"Oh, yes," answered Helen. She had been bored to pieces by them. Fifty-eight boxes of letters and lists of bandages, splints, slings, blankets, pills, and something awful called amputation saws.

"Well," said the custodian, "the four sisters ran a splendid charity during the Civil War. You know about the Great Stone Fleet of course."

"Of course," said Helen. Every schoolchild in New Bedford knew that the City of New Bedford had sent all its old whaling ships, fifty of them, laden with rocks and had sunk them in Charleston Harbor, blockading it so that the Confederate government could not get supplies in. Every New Bedford schoolchild believed that as a result New Bedford was solely responsible for the Union and Abraham Lincoln's winning the Civil War.

"Well, those four sisters," the custodian buzzed on, "knew the South was low on supplies. They knew southern boys, children of God as much as northern boys, were suffering the tortures of the damned in makeshift field hospitals. Nothing but tents, most of the time. The southern armies couldn't get any medicines at all. Young men were dying right and left of gangrene and septicemia,

screaming in agony as the few doctors they had bound
their wounds with old shirts and prayed over their agony.
I think the Fairchild sisters felt a little guilty about that
Great Stone Fleet depriving these human beings of any
comfort, and so they raised money all over town, much of
it at their own expense, and sent the southern boys all of
these things you see here in the lists. It was a selfless
Christian effort on their part and one of the many noble
acts of this fine family. The sisters devoted themselves to
charity and God's work. They were so dedicated that
none of them even married until long after the war."

Above the custodian's head was a splendid portrait of
Lorenzo Fairchild. Asa Roche's words ran through
Helen's head: "War profiteer. Made a mint off the Civil
War."

"Don't you think so?" asked the custodian.

"Oh, yes," said Helen. She stifled a yawn, and when the
custodian's back was turned, she gave the glowering face
of Lorenzo Fairchild an evil look, before she went to telephone her father. It would take half an hour, her father
said. He had to stop first at the supermarket before it
closed.

Helen settled back into her chair in the library. In a
corner wing chair the custodian had fallen asleep over his
Sunday crossword. The library was totally quiet but for
the ticking of a grandfather clock and the hissing of a
dehumidifier in the corner. In the box of pictures was one
of the gardens of the Fairchild mansion as it had been
in the year 1870. Helen looked out through the French
windows at the end of the room. The garden now was

much as it had been then. The same chrysanthemums and asters and roses filled the same oval beds. The trees had grown since then, but almost everything else, the fountain, the rose arbor, and the feeling of great wealth combined with peace, was identical. She remembered guiltily to put on the white cotton gloves as she idled through the pictures.

Some were printed on thick cardboard, some on metal, and some in ornate ebony frames looked like mirrors, as she could see both the positive and negative images, depending on how the light struck them.

The people paraded before her, stilled in their sepia landscapes, numb and distant as the moon.

In the corner the grandfather clock ticked on. Over its face was a window. A painting of the sun with a huge grin rose slowly on a metal disk in the clock's window. The clock had been there two hundred years, the custodian had told her earlier. Its sun had smiled on all these Fairchilds. It was smiling now on her, and something told her that in this silent house, which smelled of leather and lemon oil, there was an answer.

One after another she pored over the pictures. She wished she could will one grim Fairchild mouth to life and ask it to speak out about its time. She tried with all the vigor of her imagination to yank the stiff, formally posed bodies out of the photographer's chairs, out of the iron clamps that held their heads motionless for the slow glass plates that would have blurred with the slightest movement. Their time had been as full of colors and odors and noises as the day dying outside the French windows, but she could not stir a breeze that would so much as ruffle a watered-silk hoop skirt or a feathered hat. Each picture remained still and bloodless, frozen away in the land of the dead.

On the back of each picture was an inscription, neatly written by Lorenzo in the same flawless, elegant script that filled his diaries, a magnificent, strong cursive that had not been taught in any school on the face of the earth in more than a century. There was no Lucy.

The restless white gloves on her hands flicked the pictures faster. Cats, dogs, and servants, babies in wicker prams languishing on lawns and verandas now vanished. The names, the dates, the locations of summer houses on now extinct streets in New Bedford and Saratoga Springs flew by. A woman in a rowboat, her teeth just breaking a smile, was labeled *Virginia, 187?, Uncle Francis's skiff, Newport.* A very elderly gentleman in one of the mirror-like images was barely visible save for the wispy hair against an antimacassar. Lorenzo had marked it *James Madison Fairchild, 1851, old house.* A small tintype in an oval frame with a gilt mat held her attention. In it was Lorenzo, but not stern and cold as he appeared in his official portrait, where burnsides covered the wattles of his smug jowls and his hand was stuck imperially in his waistcoat. Here he was younger. His arm lay gently across the shoulders of a young girl, no more than fifteen, whose head inclined against his coat and whose face was lit with pleasure. Helen wondered who she was, as the tintype was unmarked. It could have been Virginia. Or Clara. There was a strong resemblance among all four sisters. Maybe it was Lucy, she told herself sadly, but no one would ever know, as it was unlabeled. She put the pictures neatly away and dropped the white gloves on top of the box.

The following afternoon at four, Helen cut her hand for the third time with the X-Acto knife. Under her breath she said the worst words she knew. In the pressroom lavatory was an empty Band-Aid box. Helen ran cold water on her hand for a few minutes and made her third bandage of the afternoon out of masking tape and a piece of bunched toilet paper.

While she was tending to her cut, Pinky took the flat she had been working on, which was now spattered with blood, and redid it cleanly.

"No wonder you had such an easy time getting this job away from Beverly," he joked when Helen came back. "This is slave labor."

"Jerry," said Helen wryly, "told me it was an honor to do it." She sat down heavily on her dirty, nicked, and loose-legged drafting stool. She looked for a moment at Pinky's usual drooping collar and comfortable pullover with leather patches on the elbows. The X-Acto knife, sharp as a new razor, lay waiting for her to cut more rubylith and finish up one more flat. "I wish I could just pull myself onto a soft cloud and float away," Helen said.

"Why don't you go home?" Pinky suggested. "I'll finish."

"That's okay," said Helen. "This'll just take five minutes." She knew it would take twenty. She sheared off a piece of the dark-red rubylith and plopped it down on a piece of acetate. She guessed that Jerry Rosen went through the scrap baskets when he was in one of his money-saving moods to see how much she wasted. She didn't care. She removed the stick-on backing from the rubylith and began trimming it slowly to fit the photograph of a bowling trophy. "It's like an awful dream where you keep running and can't get anywhere, Pinky," she said, yawning. "I spent twelve hours in the Fairchild mansion this weekend. Nothing. No Lucy. No Thurber. Elizabeth Fairchild was right. Asa made her up."

"Maybe you're looking in the wrong place," said Pinky, cleaning his inky thumbnail with a bent paper clip.

"Well, I wish you'd tell me where the right place is!" Helen snapped without meaning to. "I was down in that hot, moldy old mansion all Saturday and Sunday afternoon while you were sitting home in the sun. Clumsy clod, dropping that scrimshaw! Damn!" The knife slipped again. Another dot of blood fell onto a clean piece of repro under her hand.

"Keep your hair on," said Pinky.

Suddenly all the rage and fear and helplessness she felt came surging out of her, with Pinky as its target. "If you get on my hair again, Pinky Levy," said Helen, "I'll wreck your press. I'll pour ink all over it!" She wrapped her finger in masking tape and crouched over the drafting table. A whole line of type was ruined.

"Jeez Louise! It's only an expression," said Pinky. "I wasn't even thinking about your stupid hair!"

"Thanks a lot," said Helen. "If you hadn't been such a clumsy clod and dropped that scrimshaw, you would have been able to help me go through the zillion stupid letters in the stupid Fairchild mansion."

"You're tired," said Pinky tolerantly. "Better knock off

before the knife slips again and cuts off one of your enormous boobs." He caught Helen by both wrists as she dived off the drafting stool at him.

"I'll get you, Pinky Levy!" she yelled. The knife dropped and landed, point first, on the linoleum floor.

"Hey, you're strong for a girl!" he said, laughing and avoiding a kick from Helen's sneakered foot. "Think you can beat up Mr. Monster with the shiv?"

Helen's arms relaxed as her anger subsided. "I'm sorry, Pinky," she said. "I keep forgetting. You're the only one who believes me and who's helping me." She sat back down and began remaking one of the masking-tape bandages. From the doorway came a delighted chuckle.

"Have to report you for unseemly physical contact!" said Mr. Bro. Pinky and Helen laughed with him. "I've missed you," he said to Helen. "You promised to report to me, and I haven't seen hide or hair of you in a week. Except during class, and then you run like a rabbit the minute the bell rings. And by the way, Miss Curragh," he added, "I would like to be included among the select few who believe you!"

Helen yanked the knife out of the floor. The blade broke in half. "I'm afraid there's nothing left to believe," she growled, tossing the knife onto the table in disgust. "All paths lead nowhere. I'm fed up with files. Now I have to call Aunt Stella before she thinks I've fallen into a black hole in space."

When she returned, she found Pinky and Mr. Bro deep in conversation, happy as two boys trading baseball cards. "So!" said Mr. Bro. "You've learned quite a lot in your travels this week. Pinky's filled me in on the Fairchilds and Asa Roche and old Dizzy Lizzy. That the button he gave you?"

"Yes," said Helen. "It came off Lorenzo Fairchild's Civil War uniform. It's solid gold." The button hung now against her breastbone on her locket chain. Despite the fact that it had belonged to awful old Lorenzo, she liked the feel of it there—mostly because Asa Roche had given it to her.

"And you found nothing at the mansion, I take it," said Mr. Brzostoski. "No Thurbers? No missing sisters?"

"Nothing," said Helen. "Zero. And what I'm going to do, Mr. Bro, starting tomorrow, is to sneak my way into every old warehouse and building in this town and find the Thurber by myself. With Pinky," she added.

"Take it easy," said Mr. Bro. "You do that, and I'll have to call your folks. I can't let you take such a risk."

"Mr. Bro!" said Helen. "Calling my folks and stopping me isn't going to let me sleep at night. How would you like to be fourteen years old and jump every time you see a shadow or hear someone whistling because you think they'll pull a knife or an ice pick on you. Don't you understand—"

"Wait a minute," said Mr. Bro. "Just wait a minute. Maybe it's the end of the line, and I'll have to go myself to Sergeant Reynolds, but I don't think he can help us much now. I don't think the police will do a house-to-house search for this machine. I want you to tell me everything you saw in the Fairchild mansion. I smell a rat in this business about the missing Lucy. Tell me."

Helen did.

"Photographs," said Mr. Bro. "That many and some taken outdoors? In boats? On lawns?"

"Yes," said Helen wearily. "And nothing in them but a bunch of people dead for more than a hundred years."

"It's very unusual," Mr. Bro went on. "People had portraits taken in those days, sure. Lots of them. But outdoor shots? As far as I know, only Matthew Brady, the great Civil War photographer, was taking action shots or outdoor shots. That means Lorenzo was very much a lover of inventions and gadgets. Privately owned cameras were as rare as typewriters in those days. Wait a minute! Did you say that button on your chain is solid gold?"

"Yes," said Helen. She slipped it over her head. "My dad says it's gold. He bit into it. It says Third Light Horse on it and something else worn off. I haven't really looked closely."

Mr. Bro bit into the button as well and nodded. He held it under the light. "The only solid gold buttons ever made for any American uniform were for southern officers," he said, "at the beginning of the Civil War."

"Southern?" asked Pinky. "Asa said it came off Lorenzo's Union uniform."

Mr. Bro shook his head. "Confederate officers had their uniforms tailored by hand, like their suits," he explained. "Northern officers, even generals and admirals, had their uniforms issued by the government in Washington, and believe me, the government never issued solid gold buttons. Third Light Horse," he read off the button. "That would have been a mounted infantry unit. Not the sort of thing for your Lorenzo Fairchild. Now, what is this worn-off word? Starts with a *V*." He brought a pair of glasses out from his pocket and stared at it. "Valdosta," he said after turning the button around many times. "Valdosta Third Light Horse. Valdosta is in Georgia."

The silence in the drafting room was neither comfortable or uncomfortable but was charged with electricity as pungent as the smell of the furnace down the hall.

"Could it have been Lucy's husband's button?" said Helen at last. "Could he have been a southerner? The other sisters never got married until the war was over. But Lucy—if Asa Roche isn't making her up—was married. He said her father gave her a house for a wedding present."

"Go back and talk to Asa Roche," Mr. Bro said, "and ask him—"

"But Mr. Bro," said Helen, "you don't understand. Mrs. Fairchild will never let us talk to him if she thinks we want to know about Lucy. She was angry. She said Lucy never existed."

"Be reasonable with her. Tell her why you need to find the Thurber. These Yankee blue bloods are law-abiding community-minded types. She'll help you if—"

Pinky interrupted this time. "She'll send us right back to the cops," he snorted. "She hates us. She talked to us as if we just crawled out from under the sink."

"Then go back to the Fairchild mansion," said Mr. Bro softly. "Don't look for Lucy. They've hidden her carefully. Don't look for the Thurber again because that's hidden with her. Look for other people who were alive in her time. Try to find the name of a family doctor. You may find his papers in another place. Lorenzo may have used a doctor to try and get Lucy's house quarantined before he burned it."

"That's easy," said Helen. "There's heaps of letters from the other Fairchild sisters. They sent medical supplies down South during the Civil War because the southerners had no supplies at all. Kind of a good will charity called the Bedford Ladies' Aide Society. They had several letters to a doctor. . . . I forget his name."

"Find him," said Mr. Bro. "On a hunch I'm going to write to the Valdosta, Georgia, historical society and ask if they have something on an officer who was connected with a Yankee family called Fairchild. You find the doctor, and maybe through him we'll find Lucy's house, because I'm betting that's where your guy with the ice pick and the Thurber is."

Helen locked slantwise at Pinky, and then at Mr. Bro. "I don't believe it," she said. "This Fairchild family was so big, so well known and important . . . Lorenzo knew Abraham Lincoln personally. There are letters from Lincoln to Lorenzo in glass cases in the mansion. A family like that, so famous, couldn't just make a daughter disappear with no trace or birth certificate or record of any kind."

Mr. Bro leaned back and laughed. "You ever hear of Prince Albert?" he asked. "Duke of Clarence, grandson of Queen Victoria of England? He was next in line to become king one day, and if he had been king, he would have wrecked the Royal Family and the British Empire and scandalized the whole world. Look it up in the library someday."

"What happened to him?" asked Pinky.

"They got rid of him," said Mr. Bro. "Of course no one outside the family knew at the time. There was only one person who did."

"Who?" asked Helen.

"The doctor," Mr. Bro answered.

"Eat your peas, Helen," said Aunt Stella. "They're full of vitamins."

Helen pushed the peas around on her plate. Her father had not eaten one pea. *All the vitamins are cooked out anyway,* she thought, but she didn't say this, as Aunt Stella always tried so hard. She did say, "I take vitamins every morning."

"Peas have natural vitamins," countered Aunt Stella. "They absorb into the system instantly."

Helen stared glumly at the gray peas. "Daddy hasn't eaten one," she said.

"Your father would add years to his life if he would change certain of his habits," trilled Aunt Stella, "but I'm not in charge of your father. You are my responsibility!" She took a dignified forkful of the peas and ate them with a benign smile.

"Daddy," said Helen, "could you save me a trip to the library?"

"Glad to if I can," said her father, pouring beer into his glass and catching Aunt Stella's disapproving eye. "You've been spending so much time in libraries and preservation societies lately, I've hardly seen you for half a minute."

"How's your history paper, dear?" asked Aunt Stella brightly.

"Fine, Aunt Stella," Helen answered. "But it's not just a history paper. I've decided to do a new story for the *Whaler*'s contest." While Aunt Stella's attention had been glued on her father's beer glass, Helen had managed to get most of the peas on her plate into the napkin on her lap. Her father had seen this but had said nothing as he hated vegetables. "I wanted to ask you something about the British Royal Family," she began.

Her father grunted and uttered a mild swear word, as he always did when anything British was mentioned.

"Don't let the peat bog show through your toes, Paddy," said Aunt Stella, as she always did when she defended the English against the Irish. Aunt Stella was a great fan of the Royal Family. She kept a scrapbook on Prince Charles and Princess Diana's wedding, and on the mantel were two little mugs commemorating the birth of the new Prince William. She would not allow Helen's father to touch them, although he had brushed uncomfortably close a couple of times.

"Will you please not argue?" Helen asked.

"An argument is an Irishman's meat and potatoes," said her father, winking wickedly at Aunt Stella.

"For lack of anything else to eat in that God-forsaken country," Aunt Stella shot right back.

"Daddy," interrupted Helen, "what happened to Queen Victoria's oldest grandson?"

"Ho ho!" said her father, and his face turned serious under his beetling brows. "He would have been the king," he whispered conspiratorially, "but they bumped him off!"

Her father gazed happily at the chandelier above the dining room table. "He was a mental basket case, you

might put it," he went on, "with the smile of a fool and
eyes as light as a tiger's. Prince Albert was his name, and
when the queen was very old and near to dying, and his
father, Edward, was also old and very sick, for all they
knew Albert was going to be the king of England someday fairly soon. His family knew he couldn't read or write
more than a child. He also had terrible habits, which I'll
tell you about when you're older. The family believed he
was sick with a disease that he'd pass down to all his de-
scendants. They knew that having a crazy sick man on the
throne of England would ruin the Royal Family forever
and destroy the British Empire. Albert had a very nice,
sane younger brother. They wanted that younger brother,
George, to be king and to carry on the line, but of course
Albert, who was older, stood in George's way, and as the
only thing that could keep Albert from being crowned
king of England was death, they rubbed him out, very
quietly. No one knows exactly how it was done, but they
think the doctors doped him to death on the sly. After he
died, there was a big funeral with everyone tearing their
hair out and then a big wedding, where George married
the girl Albert had been engaged to, and everyone was
happy. They became King George V and Queen Mary,
and now we have commemorative jugs on the mantelpiece
and a nice comfortable family on the throne of England,
headed by a woman who wears a babushka when she
rides horseback with the President of the United States."

"Don't criticize the queen," said Aunt Stella fiercely.
"And I don't know where you get all this palaver about
murdering their own flesh and blood."

"A convenient accident," said Helen's father with a

grin as he took out a cigar. "A little too convenient. They paid off every doctor and servant and nurse who had any knowledge of it."

Aunt Stella had removed herself to the living room, away from the cigar, but she yelled back, "Just like your Ted Kennedy and the girl he did in!"

"Lay off Ted Kennedy," said Helen's father. "He's the only hope this country has!"

"He can explain till he's blue in the face but it won't bring back that family's beautiful daughter," answered Aunt Stella.

"Please!" said Helen. "Don't have another Ted Kennedy fight."

"Okay," said her father. "Now, tell me why you're writing a paper on Prince Albert of England when you're taking American history."

"It isn't on Prince Albert," said Helen. "It's on another cover-up, a hundred and twenty years ago, here in New Bedford. I think."

"You think?"

"Lorenzo Fairchild," Helen began, but her father interrupted.

"That old slave-driving robber baron," he said. "Importing innocent children and girls from Ireland and working them to death in his mills. The little ones were forced to work twelve hours a day for twenty cents. Half of them lost their fingers in his bloody Slater machines. Half of them died."

"The Fairchilds were one of New Bedford's finest families!" said Aunt Stella from the living room.

"Dad," said Helen, paying no attention to Aunt Stella,

"if I can find out that Lorenzo Fairchild somehow either killed or got rid of his youngest daughter, Lucy, if I can get to the bottom of this, I'll win a gold medal for the *Whaler*'s best story of the year. No freshman's ever won it. But I will!"

For a moment Helen wanted to tell him everything. How she never wanted to walk alone anymore. How she avoided all places with only one exit. How she peered into the bushes from her bedroom window every night looking for someone moving, looking for the glint of a knife. If she told him she was really after the Thurber machine, he would first be angry that she'd broken her promise not to cause trouble. Then tears would come to the rims of his eyes, and he would hold her close and reassure her with all the words and reasons he could find, and they would not do a particle of good. So Helen swallowed hard what was in her heart, keeping it in, keeping it down, and asked him only what was in her mind.

"Dad," she said, "if it was such a well-kept paid-off secret about the prince being . . . bumped off, how come *you* know about it?"

"Ah," said her father and blew five perfect smoke rings into the air, "because there were people who whispered, then and afterward. A servant's diary here, a doctor's paper there. Nearly a hundred years later it all came out, and people say the prince might have been Jack the Ripper. You see, babe, no matter how careful someone is, no matter how thorough, there's always something that leaks out because we are only human creatures, all of us, and the most prudent plotter in the world will still make mistakes."

Helen kissed her father and squeezed his hand tightly for a long moment, a little too long. She wondered that he didn't seem to wonder why. Then she went upstairs to face two pages of algebra equations.

The numbers and signs all blurred before her eyes. She looked out the window. Staring at her from the branch of a maple tree were the phosphorescent eyes of a cat.

Mistakes, she thought as she relaxed. She closed her eyes. *You out there, with the Thurber and the needle or the ice pick*, she whispered to herself. *Have you made a mistake yet?*

And Lorenzo, careful, thorough Lorenzo with the precise handwriting, labeling every picture like an accountant. *Every picture but one!*

"Because," she said aloud, her eyes closed with the little tintype of Lorenzo and his daughter clearly pictured in her mind, *because you couldn't label it. It was Lucy. And you couldn't throw it away either because you still loved her too much.*

Under the grainy cinnamon fog the trust and tenderness in Lucy's eyes, the care and gentleness in Lorenzo's arm laid across her shoulders were so pure and powerful that they broke out of the settlement of ghosts and into a September evening a hundred and thirty years later.

Outside the cat in the tree blinked and disappeared as quickly as a magician's trick coin, as if in fear.

NINE

Helen sat comfortably in one of the Fairchild library's leather padded chairs. *It's my lucky day,* she told herself firmly, *for once and at last it's my lucky day.* To begin with, she had passed her algebra test with an *A*, an amazing happening because she'd hardly studied the night before. The second thing was that Barry de Wolf had finally approved her Hummel drawings, but the lucky thing about that was that he was on the *Whaler* telephone when he nodded his smiling, serious approval and had not had a chance to ask her for the Hummel statue back. Aunt Stella had still not found a replacement for the chipped one that stood on her desk. After that, Jerry Rosen, with some embarrassment, had asked her for new football booster tag drawings. Apparently the principal had hit the roof at Beverly's altered faces and had demanded that they be done by one person, the person who'd drawn the bodies in the first place. And then there was Dr. Wilberforce. She had found his name two minutes after she'd opened the Fairchild sisters' file. She had checked it in several other files. Apparently the Fairchilds only consulted this one doctor. Apparently he was *the* family doctor.

She had time on her hands. Aunt Stella was to pick her up wherever she called from at five-thirty. It was only ten of four. She looked at the sweetly smiling sun above the face of the grandfather clock and smiled back. She looked also at the grim painting of Lorenzo and, when the custodian's back was turned, stuck out her tongue at him.

"May I see the photographs again, please?" Helen asked.

"Well of course, miss," came the answer. "Mrs. Fairchild herself has come by. She asked that you be given every help I can extend."

Houses. The photograph collection abounded with houses. One of them had to be Lucy's. There were ten or eleven different houses pictured. Among them were Elizabeth Fairchild's own house on Orchard Street and the mansion. The custodian knew them all.

He brought out a large map of New Bedford drawn up by the town fathers just before the Civil War in 1860. Helen held her breath. Somewhere among the crisscrossing of old roads and farmlands that no longer existed Lucy's house had to be. But the custodian pointed to every photograph and then to a tiny square or oblong on the map and identified every house that had belonged to a

Fairchild. With the exception of the mansion itself and Mrs. Fairchild's house they had all been replaced by parking lots or urban renewal housing projects, or they had fallen into the sea during landslides and storms. The custodian was not lying. Helen had lived in New Bedford all her life. The streets, the squares, the farmlands where all the other old houses had been no longer existed. Even the coastline of the shore was different.

The day was beginning to turn unlucky. She could feel that. Still, she had the doctor's name. She would call Pinky, and he would try to find the doctor's papers in the Preservation Society while she went to the public library, but the house, the house that was the key to where the Thurber lay, was hidden. The house was not on any map. She looked at three other maps of later dates. It didn't exist.

Before she put the photographs away, she looked for the little tintype, the unlabeled one, that she knew was Lucy.

It was gone.

"Everything that was in the collection is there still," said the custodian.

"But I saw it with my own eyes!" Helen said. "I can describe every detail of it."

"I'm sorry, miss. There are so many pictures. You must have made a mistake."

"It was the only one that was unmarked." Helen's temper began to flare. "It was there Sunday. It *was*."

"No one has been near the photo collection," said the custodian.

"That's a lie!" said Helen. "Elizabeth Fairchild's been here. She took it, didn't she?"

"No, miss. She only came in the parlor. Not the library."

Helen stood up. "That is a lie!" she repeated. "A lie. You are hiding Lucy Fairchild. It was her picture."

"No such person ever existed," said the custodian sadly.

"All right," said Helen, warning herself to shut up, "but I'll tell you something, and you can tell Mrs. Fairchild. I'm going to find Lucy. I'm going to find what Lorenzo did to her, and I'm going to write it up in the school paper, and the following week it'll be in the *Post-Dispatch*. I'm going to expose every lousy thing Lorenzo Fairchild did, including torturing innocent little Irish children who came over to work his mills and lost their fingers in the machinery!"

Idiot! Idiot! Idiot! she told herself. She didn't dare ask the custodian if she could use the telephone, and now she'd have to find another—heaven knows where.

Out on Orchard Street there were no telephone booths. Nor on Hancock Street, as if the presence of a phone booth in the historic district might attract the riffraff. Helen walked twelve blocks in the now chilling and swirling wind until she came to Dock Street. There she found a telephone booth. It was filled with dirty paper cups and newspaper, but at least the phone worked.

She dropped in a dime and waited patiently for the telephone down the hall from the *Whaler* pressroom to be picked up. Pinky would probably be alone. It would take ten rings before he ran up the stairway and answered it.

She watched the legs of a man who was lying half on the pavement and half under the jacked-up rear end of a car.

The man pulled himself out from under the car. He

banged his wrench against the pavement. A nut, stuck in the wrench's claw, would not come loose. He reached into a toolbox and began working at the nut with a long pointed awl. A breathless Pinky answered the telephone. Helen kept her eyes on the man. He had now sauntered up to the telephone booth and was leaning against its side with his full weight on his arms. The awl was in his right hand. He wore a navy blue ski mask that hid all his face but the eyes, and they were covered by a pair of yellow-tinted welder's goggles. He began to whistle.

"Pinky, I have the doctor's name," she said, trying to keep the trembling out of her voice. It would do no good to worry Pinky. He was too far away to help. On the other hand . . .

"Great," said Pinky. "Spell it."

"W-i-l-b-e-r-f-o-r-c-e," said Helen. The man outside was impatient. She could see nothing of his face behind the mask. He gestured with his awl for her to hurry. The awl was a steel spike with a wooden handle. His teeth when he grinned were large and as yellow as his welder's goggles.

"What's the matter?" asked Pinky. "Your voice doesn't sound right."

"Pinky," said Helen as quietly as she could, "I'm in a phone booth. Corner of Dock and"—she looked up between the swaying telephone wires—"Wharf. Get a police car here as quick as you can."

Pinky hung up the phone. Helen pretended to keep talking. She prayed the man outside hadn't heard her, as she could not hear his whistling from behind the thick glass of the telephone booth door. The wind howled around the street corner. Dock Street, lined with old tenement buildings, was entirely empty. No child came out with a yo-yo. No woman walked a dog. The man was staring at her. He kept whistling. Once he tapped on the door with the awl. The door of the telephone booth opened inward. If he wanted to, he could push it in with his enormous strength. She would not be able to hold him back.

She jabbered into the empty telephone line for five minutes. He hung, shifting his weight from foot to foot, like a gorilla waiting to be fed.

The squad car pulled up with a screech. Helen put back the phone and ran to it.

"Thank you," she heard the man say sarcastically, and as he dialed his number, she heard the whistling, for he did not bother to close the door. He whistled nasally, off-key, the shrill commercial jingle for Narragansett beer.

"What's the trouble?" asked the policeman.

Too stunned and shaking to answer, Helen leaned against the open window on the passenger side of the police car. "I couldn't . . . couldn't get the phone booth door open. I was trapped. The door stuck," she lied.

"Uh," said the policeman, "why didn't you ask him to help you?"

"He . . . he looked so scary," said Helen.

"I suppose so," said the policeman. "With the ski mask. He always wears it when he's under a car. Keeps the oil drips off his face. He's just a pussycat, though. Off-duty cop. Moonlights as a mechanic. Name's Sandy Reynolds."

The policeman offered to have Pinky, who was waiting at the public phone at school, called and reassured via the dispatcher. He then volunteered to drive Helen across town and drop her at the public library, as it was on his way. Slowly, as they drove, she stopped shaking and the color came back into her cheeks.

"Say," said the policeman, "weren't you that girl who was out on the hill after the rock thrower?"

Helen nodded.

"I'd say you have a bad case of nerves," he observed.

Helen nodded again.

"You shouldn't worry," said the policeman kindly. "Stubby Atlas is in the maximum security facility in Pittsfield. That's two hundred miles away. He won't bother you or anyone else for ten years."

"Did you ever find the little red book?" asked Helen.

The policeman shook his head. "We weren't that lucky," he answered.

"Did you ever find out the real reason why Stubby was throwing those rocks at the trucks?" asked Helen.

The policeman looked at her curiously. "He was a loony," he said. "A medically certified one hundred percent criminal. Some of them are born that way, you know. It's in the blood. In the genes."

The public library had all sorts of files on New Bedford history but Helen found no doctor's records of any kind dating before the First World War.

Pinky called right in the middle of dinner, to Aunt Stella's annoyance. The Preservation Society had nothing on doctors at all.

After dinner Helen summoned all her will. She hated, more than anything in the world, calling strangers on the telephone, but she called every Wilberforce in New Bedford. There were five. None of them had lived there for more than fifty years. None had had an ancestor who was a doctor.

Helen took a bath. She made it hot and poured half of Aunt Stella's French bath-oil beads into it. One by one she popped open the brightly colored gelatinous beads. They were like small oil-filled eggs. She kept the water running hard to cover the sound of her crying. She cried for the stolen picture of Lucy, for the unfindable doctor, for her own terror in the telephone booth, for the hours spent searching, all for nothing. There was no Thurber. There was no Lucy's house. The maps showed nothing, and if Lorenzo, as mayor, had had the maps redrawn to hide the house, he'd done well. He'd made only one mistake in not labeling the little picture, and that mistake was too long ago and it was not enough.

All of this went through Helen's mind. All the pieces that did not quite fit, like dappled bits of separate jigsaw puzzles. Then she let everything fall from her mind and cried still harder into her washcloth. This time it was not out of terror that someone was after her with a weapon. This time it was because ever since she'd been little, she'd been raised to be intelligent, to follow things through and not drop them in the middle, to use her eyes and ears and good brain and good heart, and she had failed. Was everything in the real world a lie or a trick?

Aunt Stella knocked on the door timidly. "Aren't you using a lot of water?" she asked.

"Sorry," said Helen. She shut off the tap.

"May I come in?" asked Aunt Stella. "I have something for you."

"Yes," said Helen. She wiped her face with the wash-cloth and wiggled her big toe around inside the faucet.

"You've been crying," said Aunt Stella, sitting on the edge of the tub. "Is it your gold medal article on the Fairchilds?"

Helen nodded.

"We must never count our chickens before they hatch," Aunt Stella stated. "But don't worry, dear. This will cheer you up. Here's a letter for you from Jenny down in Texas. And another thing. I found a little Hummel boy just like the one you broke."

Helen dried her hands and opened the letter. Aunt Stella opened the cardboard box. The Hummel figurine was identical to the chipped one, except the little boy held a shepherd's crook instead of a staff in his hand. "Thank you, Aunt Stella," said Helen. She did feel slightly cheered. She'd run into Barry in the library that afternoon, and he had asked her for the statue again. Otherwise she'd have to pay for it. She'd promised him she would bring it in the next morning, having no idea how she was going to keep the promise. She guessed she'd have to tell him the truth and pay for it with her hair-straightening money.

Perhaps things were not all as bad as she thought. She put failure out of her mind and looked closely at the two photographs Jenny had sent in the letter. One was of her new house with a swimming pool, and one was of herself on a horse.

"Cheer up, dear," said Aunt Stella, holding out a big, soft blue bath towel for her. "You'll write another paper. Something easier." She wound up the little Hummel music box. It was in perfect order. It played "Edelweiss," a song that Helen hated and one that her father had said was a Hitler youth anthem.

"Isn't it pretty?" asked Aunt Stella.

"Aunt Stella!" said Helen. "You know I hate those things!" But she felt better.

In bed she let her thoughts pile up pleasantly. She began to convince herself that maybe after all she had lost the locket at school. In the *Whaler* office? In the gym? While she was looking for the janitor? And maybe someone at school did have a grudge against her. A jealous freshman who thought she had gotten more than she deserved with her cushy junior's job on the *Whaler*? A jealous junior who'd wanted to do the paste-ups and the Perry and Crowe ads? She had more Perry and Crowe ads to do. Barry had given her a brochure full of Royal Doulton mice and rabbits. They would be easy to draw.

Time to get back to normal, she told herself. Jenny, down in Texas, was making new friends. She was on the school swimming team, and every day after school she got to ride horseback. Jenny missed her, but not as much as she missed Jenny.

More than anything else, now that Jenny was gone, Sister Ignatius reminded Helen of normal life. She decided she would pay Sister a visit the following afternoon. She pictured her pouring tea for them both in the spare, elegant common room of the convent. Sister's great green eyes would flash with secret jokes.

Sleep began to weigh heavily on Helen's eyelids. Faintly the image of her mother, eyeless, came to her, and faintly, as well, the image of the gold medal for Lucy's story. For an instant she pictured Stubby off somewhere in a terrible cell. *He deserves to be there,* her sensible self announced. *Yes, but so does somebody else,* a tiny faraway voice answered instantly. *Stubby is only half a story. There's another part to the crime, and I saw just a split second of it.*

Successfully Helen squeezed these thoughts and voices from her mind, because there was no hope of finding the Thurber, Lucy, the house, or the doctor. In place of these thoughts she squarely put Sister Ignatius. Sister would tell Helen all about her silliest students this year. She would say what a thing it would be if they could send their tea tray back to the kitchen on the patients' old dinner trolley from the days when the Sisters of Mercy Convent had been New Bedford's first hospital. And she would tell Helen how she'd found all this out by rummaging in the basement through papers and plans from that time.

Nothing in the night stirred, save a church bell in the middle of town. It was followed by another church bell somewhere else, as if it had waited for the first one to finish. Helen thanked God for not letting her get into trouble so far. Gratefully she promised Him and her poor dead mother, whom she imagined to be frantically worried about her up in heaven, that she wouldn't go an inch further in her spiraling search for the man in the woods. Blissfully she melted into sleep, thinking of nothing more serious than the dinner trolley high up on the

walls of the convent. She counted with the tolling bells.
One. Two. Three. Four. . . . Sisters of Mercy Convent.
New Bedford's first hospital. Papers in the basement. Doctor's papers. From over a hundred years ago. In the basement.

Sister Ignatius sat in one spindle-backed chair, Helen in
another. As Helen accounted for all that had happened
since her last visit, Sister gazed dreamily through the window and rocked back on the chair's hind legs, ever so
slightly, just the way she told her students not to do. At
last, stirring the sugar out of the bottom of her teacup, she
said, "I don't think I am any different from the other
adults who love you, Helen. I worry about where this
may lead. You may run into somebody very nasty at the
end of your search. I'm frightened. I do beg of you to
write your splendid story about Lucy Fairchild if you can,
but don't pursue this Thurber typewriter. Be satisfied with
the gold medal you will surely get for original historical
research—a pretty fish on your hook. Leave the Thurber
machine and the thug behind it to the police."

Helen nodded, not agreeing or disagreeing with this
warning, but Sister Ignatius's eyes were sharp, and her
knowledge of Helen was shrewd. "I will help you, of
course," she said. "I would do anything in the world for
you, Helen."

The convent's basement lay many steps below the
first floor. Vast, mildewed chambers bounded by low
Gothic arches, the granite green with slime and mold, led
in four directions. The room directly at the bottom of the

stairway held dishes stacked untidily on wooden shelves. There were countless plates of all sizes, cups and soup tureens of different sets. They all looked as if they'd once belonged to a star-crossed diner. They were chunky, coarse china with colored stripes on the pitted rims. Sister Ignatius paused to tinker with this collection before they went on.

Nearly an hour later they came to the vault they were looking for and the papers from St. Joseph's Hospital. Helen's hopes plummeted. The hospital had been built in 1873, eight years after the Civil War had ended. Probably about ten years after Lorenzo had asked that Lucy's house be condemned. Ten years too late. She shoved the pile of papers she was about to look through disgustedly back in a moldering box.

Sister Ignatius looked up at her over her spectacles. "I know you think we're ten years too late," she said, "but I'm not going to give up the ship. Not yet." And the reflection from her hurricane lamp, placed on an upturned sea chest, glinted like phosphorus on the gold rims of her glasses.

"See!" said Sister Ignatius. "Some of these papers go way, way back. Here's one from 1832. It's my guess that the doctors who worked here when the hospital was built left all their previous records in this basement. Here's a Dr. Pettigrew who treated a Mrs. McCarver for vapors five times in the year 1840. Wilberforce? No Wilberforce."

Helen waited for Sister Ignatius to finish off the box. The light was too dim to see more than one paper at a time, and she waited at Sister's elbow, peering over her arm at the crabbed old writing. The papers were nothing like those at the Fairchild mansion. They had putrefied over the years, suppurating filth into the decomposing boxes. Helen hoped against reason that in one of them would be Lorenzo's second mistake.

It came at the end of the very last box. Sister Ignatius was about to close it because she'd seen nothing of interest in it. What Helen saw, on a decaying sheet of paper, the middle of it literally soaking into the bottom of the box, was the word *Valdosta*. She grabbed the box.

"Wait!" said Sister Ignatius, just as excited. "Don't touch it. It's so old one touch will destroy it. Put those other papers over there, and let's bring it out into the light."

By the grim, chilly illumination of a moss-covered window they began deciphering the scratchy writing. "Doctors had terrible penmanship in those days too," remarked Sister Ignatius. They read what they could of the short paragraph, Helen holding one end of the box and Sister the other.

I have concluded an examination of Major Freder
Valdosta Light Horse. He remains in good health, b
mind and body, excepting his blindness that can
healed by the hand of God alone. He suffers this im
with courage and grace, thanking God each
that the Union shell, which exploded and cruelly robbed
him of the gift of sight did not take his life or limbs
Though he passed many months recovering his sensiblilt
despicable conditions in the swamps of Louisiana, he
shows no symptom of swamp fever, dysentery, malaria

or cholera. His personal effects and household are comp
free from contamination, thus
no quarantine is held to be necessary.

> *Duly sworn before*
> *The Magistrate, Court of Assizes*
> *County of Bristol, City of New Bedford*
> *Commonwealth of Massachusetts*
> *Roger Wilberforce, December 4, 1863*

"My God! Oh, Sister"—Helen's hand flew to her mouth in apology—"I'm sorry. I didn't mean to take the name of the Lord in—"

"Go on, Helen. What does this mean to you?"

"It means," said Helen simply, "that Lucy had the Thurber."

"How do you know that?"

"Sister, this man was blind! Lucy's husband was blind! I'd clean forgotten that Uncle Max told us the Thurber was also invented as a braille writer for blind people. The letters it printed were raised so that you could read them with your fingertips. It says right here he spent months in a field hospital in Louisiana. Lucy must have written to him there. The only way he could read was in braille, and that's why she had the Thurber!"

"I think you are right, Helen. Lucy must have owned the Thurber braille writer. You are getting very close to Lucy now."

"I still haven't any idea where she lived. Where the house was. The house Lorenzo had burned to the ground."

"Your Asa Roche was not making up a story," said Sister Ignatius. "Lorenzo did indeed trump up a reason for destroying everything. The doctor says right here there was no disease. No reason for quarantine. I wonder why Lorenzo did it? What a pity all the reasons and records and all memory have been burnt to the ground."

"All except her Thurber machine," said Helen. "That's here in New Bedford somewhere."

Sister cleared her throat. "You will get closer and closer to Lucy," she said. "I have no doubt you will find her one day, but be careful if you find her and she leads you to the Thurber, because someone else has found it first. Do you understand me? Go and discover Lucy and all the story around her. Write about it and win your medal, but don't take that last step and go after the writing machine. It's too dangerous. I implore you not to."

Sister Ignatius pressed the gangrenous wooden box deep against the front of her habit. Her smooth face broke into a clear smile of triumph, just as the sun broke through the cloud cover outside, transforming the ugly mossy windowpane into a web of translucent spring green.

Suddenly, as if they had been instructed to, Helen and Sister Ignatius both peered at the paper in the bottom of the box. They watched the free sides of it rise and curl of their own accord. Then the paper sagged and disintegrated, the whole of it now only a patch of gray dust.

Sister Ignatius whispered, "We let it into the oxygen and daylight for the first time in nearly a century and a half. It was too much." She hesitated and whispered again, "But it was alive for one moment, child, and it spoke to us!"

TEN

"Stupid, stupid, stupid. Dumb, dumb, dumb," said Mr. Bro, cracking open his fiftieth pistachio nut and sweeping a pile of shells into his wastebasket.

Helen had already read Mrs. Fairchild's letter. Pinky was in the process of reading it. In clear and animated handwriting Elizabeth Fairchild had written the principal of the school asserting that Helen and Pinky had been loud and abusive to the custodian of the Fairchild mansion, and Pinky had damaged property there.

"I just dropped an old whale tooth," Pinky complained.

"What did you call the custodian?" asked Mr. Bro.

"A . . . a fish-faced old barnacle. I could have said worse," said Pinky.

Somewhere behind Mr. Bro's stern face Helen saw the twitch of a smile. "The custodian lied to me," Helen said. "I told him I'd write up the story of Lucy."

"And blow it sky-high, right?" asked Mr. Bro.

Helen nodded unhappily.

"Well, you guys are up a creek without a paddle. I can't believe you'd be so boneheaded," Mr. Bro said, opening another nut and pushing a few across the desk for them. "You were almost there. Almost there, and now you've blown it. Blown it! You know about Lucy, you know she had the Thurber. You could have gone to Mrs. Fairchild and gotten the rest of the story from her. Believe me, she knows it. Now she'll never talk to you. And I doubt you'll find the house or the Thurber."

A wasp banged itself again and again into one of the back windows of Mr. Bro's classroom. Helen wondered why it didn't have a concussion. It had been banging for ten minutes. Mr. Bro's shoulders relaxed. "I don't blame you," he said after peering at Pinky and Helen for a curious minute. "I suppose if I were your age, I'd have called him a fish-faced old barnacle too. Let's think."

Helen allowed herself to hope.

Mr. Bro went on. "This . . . this Ladies' Aide Society. I think Lucy, with a southern husband, probably was in on that with her sisters."

"Sending all that junk down South," said Pinky.

Mr. Bro assembled a new pile of nutshells on his blotter. "Junk!" he said. "Do you have the slightest idea what conditions were like then? During the Civil War doctors used to have races to see who could cut off a leg fastest!

They had no anesthetics, nothing but morphine. That and opium were the only pain-killers in the world. You could buy them at any general store in America. But *try* having a leg cut off with just morphine! They had to strap the soldiers onto the operating tables with saddle girths to stop them from flying through the top of the tent. They had to stuff their mouths with shirt sleeves to keep down the screaming. Do you know that dentists back then, even with morphine and liquor in their patients, strapped them into chairs and pulled teeth with the head of a *key?* So don't call it junk. It was needed. Now. Get back to the point. The only thing you can do is to go back to Elizabeth Fairchild and apologize. And then see if you can make her talk to you."

"Could you," Helen stammered, "could you call her ahead and sort of calm her down first?"

"It's not *my* apology," said Mr. Bro. "It's yours!" Mr. Bro collected himself and added, "But I'll tell you just how to approach her."

The moment Elizabeth Fairchild answered the door and stood over them on the top step like an eagle examining a couple of mice, Helen forgot everything Mr. Bro had told them to say.

"I suppose you've come to apologize," she said.

"Yes," said Helen and Pinky together.

"Good!" said Mrs. Fairchild and slammed the door.

"Hatchet-faced crock of lard!" muttered Pinky to the closed door.

But Helen got down on her hands and knees on the steps and, pushing open the mail slot, yelled, "Please,

Mrs. Fairchild. We are truly sorry. Please help us." She fumbled in her pocketbook and took out her locket. She dropped it through the slot in the door. "Please look at this. Somebody sent it to me. Inside is my mother's picture. The eyes have been poked out with a needle. Someone wants to do that to me! To my eyes. I need your help!"

A minute went by. The bird-of-prey eyes peered down through the fanlight at the top of the door. "Go to the police, then, why don't you?" was Mrs. Fairchild's answer.

"They won't believe us, Mrs. Fairchild. Please just hear me out!"

Very slowly the door opened. Elizabeth Fairchild gave the locket back to Helen. But it was open. She had looked at it. "You may explain," she said. "If you take under a minute and do your explaining on the doorstep."

Helen's explanation took many minutes. During it she kept her eyes locked on Elizabeth Fairchild's. Little by little, as she told about the whistler and Uncle Max and the search for Lucy's Thurber, the patronizing steeliness melted. The stiff-necked posture relaxed.

"You should have told me all this the first time you came," said Elizabeth Fairchild.

"I tried," said Helen.

They waited in the sitting room while Mrs. Fairchild fetched tea. Once again she refused any help with the heavy silver tea service and did not talk until she had stirred lemon and sugar into her own cup and made sure they did the same.

Then she began awkwardly, tracing the pattern of a

running deer in the Persian rug idly with her shoe. "I'm a Roche, of course," she said. "Only a Fairchild by marriage. I would never have heard the story of Lucy if it hadn't been for Asa." She raised her eyes to the ceiling. "Asa was always a blabbermouth," she added. "How *he* found out I don't know, but my husband, John Fairchild, the Lord rest his soul, made me swear with my hand on the family Bible that I would never tell it." Mrs. Fairchild stopped for a moment, as if to recall that moment of swearing. "But now that you've told me about this . . . this criminal who's threatened to . . . to poke out your eyes or worse, I suppose I must break my word." She picked a tea leaf off the tip of her tongue and placed it delicately on her napkin. Pinky stared at his cup of tea. He hated tea. "That's Earl Grey tea," said Mrs. Fairchild. "Don't waste it!" Pinky swallowed about half a spoonful. Satisfied, Mrs. Fairchild continued. "I cannot in good conscience let old Lorenzo reach out of his grave with his bloodstained hands and cause any more trouble than he did during his lifetime."

"What did he do to Lucy?" asked Helen.

"Dynamited her house. Or so they say. It may be a rumor, but there was a great explosion that night. Lorenzo removed most of the valuables"—here Mrs. Fairchild chuckled—"including the gold buttons off her husband's uniform, one of which I see Asa gave you."

Helen nodded and felt the little button instinctively.

"Yes, well. Even the uniform buttons. How *terribly* cheap! At any rate, I have no idea whether Lucy died in the fire. I know her husband did. They found his body— he was blind, you see. Blinded in the war. I suspect Lucy was not in the house or else Lorenzo would never have been able to remove the valuables that afternoon. Perhaps he never intended to kill the husband—but he did. He was a murderer, Lorenzo. All I know about Lucy is that she worked shoulder to shoulder with her sisters in Bedford Ladies' Aide Society. Whatever happened to her is lost."

"Where was the house?" asked Helen.

"I don't know," said Mrs. Fairchild. "No one knows that. Lorenzo was mayor of New Bedford at that time. He not only destroyed every record of Lucy's existence but had all the town maps changed so the location of her house would be erased forever. Lorenzo was a very methodical man."

Helen had finished her tea. Her cup was empty. The Persian rug was deep and soft, and the cup did not break when she dropped it.

"Dear child!" said Mrs. Fairchild and was at Helen's side in an instant, her hand tentatively patting Helen's back, as if Helen were a puppy who'd choked on a bone. "My dear, don't cry. Crying helps nothing. I wish I could help you. I would do anything to help you, but I simply do not know where her house was."

"Thanks anyway," said Pinky. He picked up Helen's cup and saucer.

Helen steadied herself just to be polite. She took the teacup from where Pinky had put it on an antique cherry-wood drum table and set it back on the silver tray, where it wouldn't make a wet ring.

Mrs. Fairchild had settled herself in an armchair, as if nothing had happened. "I wish more than anything in the world I could help you," she repeated, "because I have something to ask of you."

Here it comes, thought Helen. She said nothing.

"If you write up this story," said Mrs. Fairchild, "and I can't stop you after all, our family will be remembered for evil and not for all the good we have done in this town. It will appear first in your school paper, and then, as you said in the mansion, it will be picked up in the Sunday supplement of the *Post-Dispatch.* Helen, is it?"

Helen nodded.

"Helen, you have a long life ahead of you. I have only a few years and Asa little time at all. Reporters will badger us, because the family is an important one. People will not leave us alone. I have a heart condition. I don't think I could bear the questions and the scandal this would cause. Please keep this story away from anyone else until Asa and I both pass on."

At the door Mrs. Fairchild pressed the little tintype of Lucy and Lorenzo into Helen's hands. She touched Pinky's sleeve and looked at them both brightly, trustingly, more like a wren than an eagle. "There's a dear," she said to Helen, holding both Helen's hands over the portrait with her own and with great warmth.

That evening Pinky was invited to dinner for the very first time. Aunt Stella watched him the way a cat watches a canary. Pinky contentedly downed two platefuls of homemade lasagna and asked for more. He even ate the edges, which were so hardened by their trip into the oven that Helen decided he must have teeth like razors.

Cheerfully and with care Pinky filled Helen's father and Aunt Stella in on all the details of their visit to Elizabeth Fairchild, except of course for any mention of the Thurber or why they wanted to find Lucy's lost house. When he came to Mrs. Fairchild's begging them not to write the story at least until she was dead, Helen's father snorted loudly, almost gleefully.

Aunt Stella let her knife fall on her plate with a clank. "Helen will of course be good and charitable," said Aunt Stella, looking warily in Helen's direction. "She has never had a mean bone in her body and I'm certain will not break this poor woman's heart in order to win herself a gold medal. She is not a Judas who would betray her nature for thirty gold medals."

Helen said nothing. The lasagna stuck to the roof of her mouth.

Her father looked at her just as warily. "You *are* going to write this splendid story, aren't you?" he asked.

Everyone waited for Helen to speak. At last she washed down the lasagna and said, "I don't know, Dad."

"You don't know!"

"Dad, it was a big thing for Mrs. Fairchild to break the promise she made to her husband. She has a heart condition. I don't want her to have a stroke or a seizure because of me."

"Stroke!" he trumpeted. "She's faking. She's only broken her promise because you two came up with some evidence. The old bat's probably terrified she'll die and not get into heaven if the Fairchild family name is ruined. That's why she asked you to wait until she dies. She figures she'll squeak past Saint Peter, and then it'll be all right. You don't get banished from heaven once you're in. That's what she's betting on."

"Duncan Curragh," said Aunt Stella sharply. "Heaven is not like your Boston Red Sox, where you look over your shoulder to make sure they don't send you down to the minor leagues. Heaven is a state of grace, as you well know!"

"Not to the bloody Anglicans, it isn't," he snapped. "Their idea of heaven is a bloody yacht club with no Catholics or Jews or Hindus allowed. They may let the good Lord run the place, but you can believe me they make Lorenzo Fairchild and his sort chairman of the board."

"The child is being wise and charitable, Duncan," said Aunt Stella. "Button your lip." Then Aunt Stella asked if Pinky would be so kind as to bring some of his mother's Norwegian recipes with him when he came over to pick Helen up for the Wareham game the next day.

Helen's father glared at her. "Doofus," he said. "You're being a bloody doofus if you don't write that story, that's all."

Pinky volunteered to do the dishes with his sweetest smile. Aunt Stella agreed to let him take Helen to the movies. "A movie will cheer you up," he whispered to her over the lasagna dish, even though he knew it wouldn't.

Aunt Stella fussed over them at the door and said it looked like rain and didn't they want to take an umbrella. Helen put the umbrella back in its stand, and she and Pinky ran down the slate walk to catch the approaching bus, but Aunt Stella's voice trilled after them.

"Yes, Aunt Stella?" said Helen wearily. They would

now miss the bus. They had been warned about everything from purse snatchers to drunken drivers running red
lights. "Something in the mail for you today!" Aunt Stella
waved a manila envelope under the porch light. "From
Georgia!" she added, as if to say Afghanistan.

A late summer moth flapped wildly against the yellow
light on the porch. The photocopy in the envelope was too
illegible to make out in the dimness.

Helen took it inside. She stared at it without speaking.
She felt as if she had lifted up a giant rock and was about
to peer under it.

Impatiently Helen's father took the copy from her
hands and, holding it under the dining room chandelier,
began to read.

"It says here," he said, " 'Dear Miss Curragh: At Mr.
Brzostoski's request we are writing to you about Lucy
Fairchild de Vivier. Sorry it took us so long to find her.
Her married name, de Vivier, is how we all remember her
down here.' " Her father paused and then went on to the
newspaper article reproduced in clotted black print on the
photostat. "From the Valdosta *Clarion*, April 5, 1911:

> Mrs. Lucy de Vivier, one of Valdosta's most be-
> loved citizens, passed away in her sleep last
> night, at her home on Lee Street. Mrs. de Vivier
> shunned the limelight all her life but was called
> "the Angel of Shenandoah" by General Stone-
> wall Jackson for the part she played in his
> great victory there.
>
> Fearing discovery and hanging for treason to
> the Union cause, Lucy de Vivier shipped over
> twenty thousand rounds of ammunition and

seven thousand Enfield rifles to our brave boys in grey. Working out of a hidden basement at the end of a private railway line in New Bedford, Massachusetts, "Miss Lucy," as affectionate Valdostans called her, sent arms secretly to our troops for over two years. Believed to have been cast out by her Yankee robber baron father, whose name was Fairchild, she never revealed her past to her many friends in town. She was the wife of Frederic de Vivier, major, Valdosta Third Light Horse, who distinguished himself and his regiment at the Battle of Shiloh. Miss Lucy chose to spend the rest of her life here, in her departed husband's home town.

May Miss Lucy rest in peace forever in the proud and grateful hearts of all Valdostans, this brave and unsung heroine of the War for Southern Independence.

There was a silence following the reading, broken only by the violent rattling of Pinky's imagination, which Helen alone could hear.

"You can write your story now," said Helen's father. "Your Elizabeth Fairchild has nothing to fear, Sweet Pea. Leave out the part about the husband dying in the fire if you wish. Lorenzo may not have intended that. But he saved his daughter's life, didn't he? She was a traitor to everything he believed in, she stole Union Army weapons, and she would have been hung or shot for it, so he wiped out every trace of her and let her go in peace to the South."

"He did?" Helen said, then added in a murmur, "A house, with a basement, at the end of a railroad line that no longer exists."

"Where has your lovely brain gone to?" asked her father, impatiently slapping his thigh. "Lucy was running guns to the enemy, smack in the middle of New Bedford, one of the biggest Union strongholds in the war. If she'd been found out to be a spy—worse than a spy, a collaborator—she'd have been put in front of a firing squad for high treason! And every widow and mother and sister and lover in the state of Massachusetts who'd lost a young man in the South would have gladly pulled the trigger on her.

"Lorenzo gave her safe passage down to Georgia. Then he wiped out every shred of her memory so she could live the rest of her life as Lucy *de Vivier,* not Lucy Fairchild. He made sure no one knew what she'd done so she wouldn't have to live out her days in fear someone would sneak up behind her and shoot her."

"I understand, Dad," said Helen, but she was repeating his last words to herself, *Sneak up behind her. Sneak up behind her.*

Aunt Stella stood in the doorway and waved good-bye under the same tireless flapping moth. As she did, she sighed and said, "Who would have thought they took the Civil War quite so much to heart down South?"

Squares of light from the streetlamps flickered onto Pinky's face, a mask of urgency.

"They've been microfilming the files every night for a week in the Preservation Society. They started when I was looking for the doctor's papers. Let's hope they're still open," Pinky said.

"If Oliver Jenkins isn't there," Helen asked, "do you know where to find the railroad maps?"

Pinky nodded. "I think so. In one of the big flat wooden drawers on the back wall. The railroad spur!" he went on and pounded his fist like a ballplayer into his other hand. "If only I'd remembered. I remembered the indoor plumbing, the gas lamps, the oil refining, even the long pants Asa told us about. But I forgot the railroad spur. I guess maybe because I didn't believe there really was a Lucy's house till now."

Helen gazed at the photostat of the Georgia newspaper. There was a picture of Lucy on it; the face was half eclipsed by bad printing, but the same mesmerizing black eyes that had glowered at her from Lorenzo's official portrait stared back from this very elderly Lucy. The same determined mouth, only on a woman's face. Helen felt a small rush of air, soft as a sigh. Through the screen that divides the dead from the living Lucy slipped without warning. For a tick of a second her eyes held Helen's, lively as a heartbeat, and seemed to signal her desperately. But was it to keep going or to keep back?

Oliver Jenkins had not been pleased to allow Pinky and Helen into the file room after hours and while the photographers were busy microfilming all New Bedford's written records. He had said he was going home to dinner and bed, and if anything was damaged or out of place, he'd call the principal of the high school on Monday morning and see to it no students were ever again allowed in the file room.

Helen and Pinky loaded the big oak table with railroad maps. On the end wall of the room a clock in an oak case ticked loudly and made a whirring noise every time its big hand advanced. The photographers making microfilm in another room clicked and thumped and buzzed away. A fire engine squealed by outside, and the light patter of rain drummed on the windows.

"Remember," said Helen, "we have only until ten o'clock. Dad'll be in front of the theater on the dot."

Half an hour ticked by on the clock in the oak case.

"It's only a maybe," Pinky reminded her. "We may find nothing. But I'm betting old Lorenzo would have had to have an army of printers to change the maps of the railroad company itself. *They* built the spur line, and they would have put it on their maps."

Finally he found a chart of the eastern seaboard entitled *New York, New Haven, and Boston. Central Railroad Projected Lines and Service*. The title was lettered in shaded brown calligraphy, handsome and perfect. The brown crosshatching showed the railroad as it existed in 1859, just before the Civil War. The track came up from somewhere south of New York City, ran north, hit New Haven, and curled up the coast to Providence, Boston, and beyond to Maine. A spidery branch ran eastward from Providence to New Bedford and on to Woods Hole at the shoulder of Cape Cod. There was no familiar canal at the beginning of the Cape. Not for fifty years more would there be one. Helen bent over the map. The lines were distorted by creases in the paper. She shook her head in exasperation. "Pinky, go see if they have a magnifying glass in there. Maybe a pair of glasses, anything!"

Pinky returned after a lot of irritated discussion with the photographers. In his hand was a round convex lens. "They want it right back," he said.

Helen held it under her eye above New Bedford on the map. The lens blurred everything to extinction except in its very middle, and there, leading straight from the center of town up into the woods where Route 6 had been built a hundred years after the map had been drawn, ran a short spur line. At the end of the line was a tiny ink oblong labeled *F.CHILD*.

"Is it enough, Pinky?" Helen asked as he squinted down through the lens. "Can you find it in the woods?"

"It's very near where you chased him," said Pinky. "We'll find it."

The photographers began shutting up shop for the night. One red-bearded man looked curiously at Helen and Pinky as he wheeled three klieg lights through the room and up a ramp. "You gotta leave now too. We gotta lock up!" he yelled.

Helen and Pinky sat, gazing wide-eyed at each other across the table, as if only they could hear the strings and woodwinds of some invisible orchestra.

"Damn!" said Pinky when they'd walked out into the rainy street. "We should have taken Stella's umbrella. What's your father going to say when he sees us come out of the movie soaking wet? We'll have to wait for him outside the marquee in the rain."

Helen popped a quarter into a newspaper vendor. They spread the *Post-Dispatch* above their heads, each holding a side.

The rain spattered in torrents all around them. It poured in swift gulleys down the gutters and sluiced fiercely out of the eaves of houses like a running bath.

The streetlights hovered eerily in oval white mists. Ahead were the red parking lights of the photographers' van.

Hand in hand Helen and Pinky walked toward the movie theater under the soggy canopy of the evening paper. Helen fretted over how many hours she could get away with being in the woods the next day. Pinky muttered his mental maps of trails and deer paths.

It began suddenly, as if someone had set off an alarm. "Climb Every Mountain" was the name of it. Helen had heard it a hundred times on the radio, in stores. Now it came from just around the corner, a throaty double-note whistling, pure as an oboe.

Helen dropped the newspaper. Pinky had already bolted in the direction of the whistling. Helen followed him, and together they hit an enormous black, dense shape. There was a sound like a Christmas ornament breaking. A voice rang out. "Stupid, clumsy kids! You've broken my bulb! That's a hundred-dollar klieg light you busted. Never think of anybody but yourselves!"

Pinky tried to disentangle himself from the wires and the legs of a tripod. It was too late. The photographer marched off yelling, "Stupid, clumsy kids!"

The dim window lights of Perry and Crowe illuminated a selection of porcelain farm animals behind the steel security grilles. Helen and Pinky stood on the corner, shedding water like statues in the park, trying to listen through the clamorous tucketing rain, but the whistler had vanished into a maze of side streets up ahead.

ELEVEN

"I hope you're not thinking of going to a football game on a day like this," said Aunt Stella, peering into Helen's room and seeing her at the window.

Helen's thoughts were not on football. They were far in the woods where Pinky and she were going to find Lucy's basement. "It's the biggest game of the year, Aunt Stella," she said.

"I don't care if it's Notre Dame playing Harvard," said Aunt Stella. "You're staying home, and that's final." She flounced down the stairs muttering about Helen's coming home last night as wet as an eel.

Helen pressed her forehead against the cold pane. Angry tears seeped out of her eyes. Pinky, free Pinky would not have to stay home. He would go and do a little exploring on his own in the woods. She knew it. She fought the tears, but they were as unstoppable as the rain outside.

Pinky, dressed to the gills in surplus Navy gear, ambled up the front walk at noon exactly. Once in the house, he shook himself off like a Labrador retriever. "Bad news," he said before Aunt Stella could make a suggestion about the Monopoly set she'd dragged out of the closet. "No football game today. At least no game for Helen and me."

"Well, I should think not," said Aunt Stella. "Come in and have some blueberry muffins and cocoa."

"Wish I could," said Pinky seriously. "Sorry, Aunt Stella. We've got an emergency at the *Whaler*." Helen had just come down the stairs. "You know all those flats you pasted up last week?" Pinky asked.

"Yes," said Helen. "What about them?"

"All pasted up wrong," said Pinky. "Jerry Rosen is furious. You have to do the whole job over today in four or five hours or you're off the *Whaler*. You have to pay for the wasted materials. Come on. My mom's getting the car gassed up at Hobson's down the street. I'll go help you with them."

Helen turned the color of cream.

"That is very nice of you, Pinky," said Aunt Stella. "Helen, I *knew* your other work would suffer because of all this galavanting around to historical societies. This is a disgrace! You'll have to pay the *Whaler* back out of your own allowance."

Helen pulled on her boots and rain gear with angry jerks. Aunt Stella passed Pinky a bag of blueberry muffins in case they got hungry. "That's what happens when you think you're too good for a job," she huffed at Helen. "And don't you start up crying again as you've been doing this past hour."

If there'd been a roll of industrial-strength nylon-reinforced packer's tape around, Helen would have pasted a strip of it over Aunt Stella's mouth.

She followed Pinky miserably out the door, stamping in every puddle on the walkway, kicking a stone across the street.

"These are very heavy for blueberry muffins," said Pinky, twirling the bag. "She must use steel blueberries."

Helen didn't answer. She wished New Bedford would be invaded by boa constrictors. She wished twenty of them would wrap themselves around Jerry Rosen's throat.

"Where's your mom's car?" asked Helen when they had arrived at the gas station. Pinky handed Helen the muffin bag. He opened a small umbrella that was lying on a stack of tires and whipped a plastic sheet off his motorcycle. "Get on," he said.

"But we can't go to school on this," said Helen. "We have to go through the middle of town and—"

"We're heading for the woods," said Pinky.

"But the flats! What about Jerry?"

"Lies. All lies," said Pinky, grinning. "I knew Stella'd never let you out of the house for a football game on a day like this. I figured the only chance to get you out of there was to use a little guilt. Guilt and shame always work."

Pinky ran the motorcycle over the edge of the curb and onto a sandy path that ran alongside the road. Helen sat behind him, holding the umbrella over both of them. She was happy. Amazed and speechless and happy for several minutes, until the houses thinned. She felt a growing cramp and weakness in her gut. Supposing *he* was up in the woods too? Supposing he was following them? She glanced back down the highway. No cars were in sight. Still she began to think she should call someone. Mr. Bro or Sister Ignatius. Just in case. "Could we just stop at a gas station?" she asked Pinky. "I have to go to the bathroom."

"Jeez Louise," said Pinky. "Wait till we get to the woods. You can go in the woods. I go in the woods all the time."

"You're a boy."

"There's not *that* much difference."

"There's a *huge* difference!"

Pinky pulled over to a small, run-down gas station. "Oh, all right," he growled. "Girl's have bladders like mice."

Helen tramped off. "Just because I'm not like some man who goes against the side of a tree like a dachshund!" she shot back.

"Think of the Indian women!" Pinky trumpeted. "The woods was all they had!"

Helen did not think of the Indian women. She was looking for a telephone. She could see that the gas station had long been abandoned. The ladies' room door hung ajar on one creaking hinge. Grass grew in cracks in the pavement. The telephone had been ripped out of the wall and hung uselessly on its cable.

She went back to Pinky and got on the motorcycle again. "There's a dead rat in the toilet," she said. "I'll use the woods." In the deserted office she had thought she saw something move. But how could anything move in an abandoned office? Her world was too full of shadows, and she was afraid of every one. She ignored the common-sense voice that told her, *Turn back. Wait until Monday. Let Mr. Bro call the police. Let the police find the Thurber.*

In a way Pinky seemed to read her thoughts. "If we find the Thurber," he said gleefully, "it'll be full of finger-prints. Nothing like a typewriter for fingerprints."

"Do you think the cops will listen?" asked Helen. "Do you think they'll come?"

"Are you kidding?" Pinky answered. "That basement's got to be chock full of Civil War guns and ammunition. If they don't come for the fingerprints, they'll sure as hell come for the guns. They're not going to leave hundreds of guns and bullets up there for some nut to use."

Helen was about to argue the point when she became aware that the ride was no longer so bumpy and that the branches were too high off the ground to reach and throw rainwater at them, as they'd done in the lower scrub woods.

The narrow trail twisted and wove around vine-threaded ashes and oaks, all the different leaf colors muted in the lime-green haze.

"This is it," whispered Pinky almost reverently. "This is where the tracks ran."

Helen wondered how long ago it was that the old ties had been prized up. Lorenzo himself must have had it done. If a rattling locomotive had ever disturbed the peace of this woods with its spewing black smoke, there was no echo or sign of it now. The rain had stopped, and the woods were dead quiet, as if in waiting for the birds to come out. Helen recognized the path. She had veered off it to hide under the stump. He had strode along the path whistling.

Pinky stopped the bike, not far from the stump, and hid it. "We have to get as far as that cliff up there," he said, pointing. "That's where the map shows the site of the house."

Deeper into the woods they walked. They could see a short six inches ahead. That was all. A warm, dense ground fog had followed the rain. It thickened by the second until it wrapped them and everything in the woods to the tops of the trees in an endless silver-green mist. Pinky's eyes darted and squinted, trying to make sense of the surroundings. Helen felt his hand close over hers reassuringly, but no electricity or pleasure emanated from it into her. There was only the listening, the utter concentration on the sounds in the woods, and like the trees the sounds were hidden all around them.

The rock face was just as she remembered it the day of the accident, covered with nettles and poison ivy. Pinky didn't seem any more anxious to touch it than she. They circled the ledge for a time until Pinky found a foothold and they were able to hoist themselves to the top of it.

"Perfect site for a house," said Pinky expertly. "Good view. Good foundation rock." He pulled a heavy trowel out of his slicker pocket, handed it to Helen, and using an identical one himself, began to dig. "There should be a floor under here," he said. "I bet there was an access depot to the rail line down there against the face of that rock somewhere. I'd look for it except for that poison ivy."

Helen scraped away at various points. They were enclosed by a circle of fog. Below them only the tops of some juniper trees showed above the blanket of mist. God did not feel close by. Nor did her mother. The fog would protect them, she reckoned. If anyone came, they could hide in it quickly. Lucy, who had been so close last night, was now no nearer than God. She did not guide Helen's hand or linger at her side. She had been there only for the time it takes a star to wink. Then she'd gone back.

Pinky struck bedrock four inches beneath the sandy soil in ten widely scattered places, Helen in six. He tore a limb from a tree, sheared off the twigs, and hammered it deeply into soil with a rock. The branch broke. He tried again with another and then another. He cleared the earth from several holes he and Helen had made. There was no floor, no foundation, no cellar. There was nothing but granite, old as the crust of the earth itself, laced with flaking layers of mica, thin as airmail paper.

Swearing, Pinky leaped down off the ledge. Helen could only hear him, as he was hidden from her in the fog. She knew what he was doing. He was tearing, barehanded, at the nettles and poison ivy, looking for the door in the rock face he was sure was there.

"Pinky, don't!" she cried out. The nettle thorns were sharp as darts and half an inch long. They would rip his hands to shreds, and the poison ivy would infect him three times as viciously.

There was no answer from Pinky. Only the snap of

briers crushed beneath his boots and angry groans from between his clenched teeth. "Pinky, stop!" she called again, but he went on and on.

Finally he pulled himself back to the top of the rock. "It *has* to be here," he said. "The map *showed* it was here." He kicked a clump of soaking moss down over the edge of the precipice and sat down, leaning over his folded arms and biting furiously at a hangnail.

"Well, it isn't," said Helen bleakly. "I guess it's the end for us."

Pinky did not seem to hear her. Gently she placed her hand on his shoulder. "It's so very quiet here," she said. She looked into the delicate fog-filled treetops around them. Only the crests of the dozen junipers showed above the mist like volcanic islands pointing out of a gray sea. "Pinky, thank you," she said before she'd had time to think out anything to say. "You've been with me all the time. Nobody really helped me but you."

Pinky's two fists, crisscrossed with bleeding scratches that went up over his wrists, were curled tightly in rage. He wept noiselessly, his whole body heaving with the effort, into his sleeve.

Only in the movies, thought Helen, *do people know what to say and have it all come out right.* She wanted to put her arms around him, but she didn't dare. She wanted to say something that would make him put his arms around her, but she didn't know how.

It didn't matter. She heard her own voice crackle through the air like sudden lightning: "Pinky, my God! Look at that!"

TWELVE

Helen jumped down from the top of the rock face, landing in a nest of briers. Pinky followed. "What?" he asked three times. "I don't see anything!"

"You can't see it now," said Helen. "You can't see it except from up there, and even then, if it hadn't been for the fog, I never would have noticed."

They crossed the grassy path again, but Helen ran on to the right of it. She stopped when she reached the first juniper tree. She slapped its rough trunk. "They were all planted, Pinky," she explained breathlessly. "All at one time. Trees in the woods don't grow naturally in a perfect square, all exactly the same height. I never would have noticed from the ground, there's too many other trees in the way. It was the fog. It blocked off every other tree below them, and only the juniper tops showed!" She paused for a little air. "Look. They must have been planted to disguise the location of the foundation of the house. It's Lorenzo's last mistake, Pinky. All of it's overgrown, but we'll find the basement here somewhere."

Very slowly Pinky approached one of the junipers, looked at the others, and calculated. As he did, he shook the wet leaves of a pokeberry plant over his wounded hands and washed them in the rainwater, grimacing with pain. "If it is here," he said, "we'll still have a job finding it. These trees have had a hundred and twenty years to set their roots."

Sometime later they found a rusty spring which could have come from a two-hundred-year-old chair or a ten-year-old chair. Then Pinky began digging around what he said looked like a hand-hewn granite block. They found a charred board and under that the beginnings of a brick walk. Helen looked carefully at the undergrowth that covered the woods floor. "Myrtle," she said.

"What?" Pinky asked.

"Myrtle. This dark-green, shiny plant. It has purple flowers in late spring. We have it at home in our garden. It's a cultivated plant, not a wild one." Breaking out of a mound of piny humus was a stand of fragile purple toadstools. Next to them was a jungle of honeysuckle and more myrtle. It grew over an oblong stone.

In the stone was a rusted iron bar, a slide bar, and under the vines was a door.

The honeysuckle and myrtle had been carefully matted

by hand to form a wild rug. Once the rug was lifted, the door into the ground opened easily.

Pinky drew a flashlight from his pocket. He jabbed the button five times, but it produced only a dim, wavering beam. He said an angry word to it.

"Batteries probably got wet," said Helen. "Never mind, I can still see." But her own words hung in her mind. *I can still see. I can still see.* She had thought a shadow had glided by one of the fog-blanketed junipers. She covered her eyes with her hands. Her eyes were so precious. Her hands too weak to . . . *Stop it*, she told herself. *I've been telling myself I've been followed for weeks now, and what does it turn out to be? A bag lady with a pair of discarded sneakers. An off-duty cop waiting for a public phone. A rabbit, a cat.*

But what was the shadow? There are no shadows in a fog.

The door into the earth led to a flight of steps which gave way to a flagstone floor. The basement spread ahead, far beyond where they could see, but smack in the middle of the room, with a chair pulled out in front of it, was the Thurber writing machine.

They turned to each other for a delighted moment but had no words. Pinky reached out and touched one of the smooth wooden keys, as if to make sure it was real, and drew back in awe. Helen unhooked the metal fasteners on Pinky's slicker and opened the stiff rubber front of it like two doors. She clasped her arms around his back and buried her face in the fuzzy pullover that was now nearly as familiar as her own clothes. At last she could speak. "The Thurber . . . it's beautiful!" was all she could think to say. "I never thought it would be beautiful!" Her eyes would not leave the burled walnut case with the word *Thurber* inlaid in mother-of-pearl below the typing keys.

"Before we go," said Pinky, "I want to take a sample of the type to show the cops. Do you have any paper?" Above them a dead twig snapped. Then another. They both looked up at the same moment. The mat of vines that had covered the basement door rustled. The door dropped back into place, clanging, then echoing. The bolt was replaced, and the footsteps ran off through the soft fallen pine needles as quickly as they had come, leaving Pinky and Helen in a blackness denser than any night.

Helen sank to her knees and felt the slimy stone floor with both hands, as if the earth itself would suddenly fail her and she would be left dangling in space.

"We're going to die, Pinky," she said.

"No, we're not," Pinky answered in a whisper. "We're not going to die." He turned on the meager glimmer of his flashlight and then shut it off again. "We're not going to die," he repeated.

Helen held Pinky's legs. Panic swarmed through her body, covering her with sweat as cold as the floor's, stopping her breathing, again turning the insides of her gut to hot, sickly water. Pinky's legs were trembling. "Are you as scared as I am?" she asked.

Through the darkness, thick as a pillow, she heard his usual ironic grin around his answer. "Hold on to it," he said. "There's no john down here."

She relaxed one or two degrees.

"Come on," said Pinky. "Let's get that door open again before he comes back."

"The bolt," she said hopelessly. "It's solid iron and embedded in rock."

"The hinges," said Pinky, "are what we'll work on."

He stumbled over to the steps, climbed them, and pointed the tiny beam of his flashlight at the bottom of the door. "If I'm right," he said, "this cellar's got to be full of old guns and ammunition. All I need is a pistol I can load, and I'll shoot off these hinges in two seconds. Even a bayonet would do. I can pry 'em out."

After many minutes of fumbling along unseen walls, over shelves, and among the shapes of unknown objects Helen found a small waxy cylinder, felt at the end for a wick, accidently broke off the wick, and then restored it, digging at it with her fingernail. They lit the candle with one of the two dry matches in Pinky's pocket. They could see quite well by it, as their eyes had now adjusted to the darkness.

Helen stared at one side of the cavernous room, Pinky at the other. Along her wall there were rows and rows of heavy woolen greatcoats, hung five deep on iron rods, as they might be in a dry cleaner's. They were huge, of a military cut, and spangled with motes of mildew. Under them were piled heaps of blankets, but for fear of spiders Helen touched neither the coats nor the blankets.

On the other side of the room Pinky was furiously scattering a supply of crutches of all sizes. Carefully rolled swaths of heavy cotton cloth fell to the floor as he searched for a gun.

Bandages, thought Helen and picked one up and put it back on the shelf.

Pinky grabbed a piece of smooth, solid wood, thin and

rounded at the ends. There were many like it. "A splint," he said. "Might be able to pry with it if it's hardwood." He set it aside and went on, yanking stethoscopes with gum-covered cloth tubes and earpieces as big as silver dollars down onto the floor. Slings, braces, sticking plaster, and a scalpel all followed. A bottle fell onto the stone beneath their feet, and the odor of camphor filled the air.

This cellar hasn't been disturbed in over a hundred and twenty years, thought Helen. Aloud she said, "There aren't any guns down here, Pinky. Lucy sent all the guns down South. This is where she stashed the medical supplies she was *supposed* to be sending in those packages. She hid it all down here."

Pinky just mumbled something about bullets and rifles. The rest of the shelves held square wooden boxes. Pinky ripped open four of them, using the splint to pry up the nails, but they were only filled with something called Dover's Powder. In the next lot were red glass flasks laid on their sides in sawdust. The splotchy labels read *Laudanum, Cure for All Maladies and Distempers of the Human Body*. There were three cartons of these. Pinky threw down his splint in disgust.

Helen took the candle and wandered to the very back of the basement, where she found a walk-in closet. Two canvas stretchers with ornately carved wooden lifters stood against the door, which creaked as she opened it. The closet's ample shelves were loaded with Dr. Theodore's Elixir, good for horse and man alike, bars and bars of oil-paper-wrapped lye soap, containers of pills, which Helen rattled against her ear, labeled in German. She picked up a round tin can, brought it close to her eyes, and read: *Dr. Buckland's Scotch Oats Essence. Cures Insanity, Paralysis, Brain Softening, Nervous Exhaustion, Sick Headache, Sleeplessness, and St. Vitus' Dance.* She put it back on the shelf. There were vials of Kidney Wort Cure, jars of Congress Water, and packages and packages of Cuticura Anti-Pain plasters.

"Anything?" Pinky called.

"Horse liniment," said Helen, "and more horse liniment. No guns, no pistols or ammunition, not even a bayonet."

"Let's not waste any more of the candle," he said, and cupping the bright little flame in his hand, he took it up the stairs and set it in a crack on the top step. Then he began to clean the rusty hinges with the scalpel.

"How long?" asked Helen, sitting on the step below him.

"I don't know. If I had a crowbar . . ." He wiped the scalpel's curved blade on his pants. Then they heard a scratching on the other side of the door.

Helen grabbed the candle. Soundlessly they hurried back down the stairs. Above them they heard the sound of metal scraping stone. Pinky looked desperately in all directions. "The coats!" he whispered hoarsely. "Hide in the coats! One in the back of the row. Button the coat first. Then get in and hide your feet under one of the blankets."

The iron door fell open with a harsh, vibrating crash. Inside the thick woolen coat Helen imagined the bluish daylight flooding into the cellar. She tried not to think of spiders and snakes and fungus in the sleeves of the coat. She could sense Pinky breathing beside her in the next coat. She remembered the smashed camphor bottle. She wished she'd taken one more second to pick up the long broken neck of it. It would have been something to hold. It was jagged and sharp. *Dear God,* she began to pray, *if You were ever by my side, please be here now. Don't let him find us, dear God. I know I have failed you many times. Forgive me. Don't let him find us.*

A quiet minute spun by. What was he doing? The person in her mind's eye was hooded, the face blank except for bright close-set eyes, like a sewer rat's. There was a pinging of glass from the far side of the cellar.

Did he have a knife? An ice pick? The scalpel! Had Pinky left the scalpel, sharp as a new razor, pointed as sewing scissors, on the top step? Had *he* found it? Slowly, without a sound, Helen turned around inside the coat. *If he stabs quickly, he'll get the back of my head,* she told herself. *Not my eyes. Not my eyes first.*

The footsteps padded to the closet. She heard the door ratchetting open and the stretchers shifting. She heard his hands moving, fingering things on shelves, shoving them slightly. She could hear him breathing in and breathing out.

Then, starting at the far end of the row, he began poking at the coats. Brass buttons clinked together as he did this. Halfway down the row he said, "Hunhh," as if he were about to stop. Then he continued. Pinky and Helen were in the next to last coats on the end.

Suddenly Pinky nudged her hard. She turned. "Run for it!" he said, his voice shattering the deep silence, but it was too late. The man had opened the buttons of Helen's greatcoat and stood directly in front of her. The light from the open door spilled behind him, and she could see nothing but his black, shadowy form. He was tall. He chuckled.

Pinky grabbed him from behind, yanking him backward off his feet. The scalpel blade in Pinky's hand flashed by like a tiny scimitar. Then Helen saw who it was, and so did Pinky, and he stopped the scalpel just short of the vein in the throat.

"What are you doing here!" Pinky yelled, straddling his chest and still not releasing him.

The old Indian sputtered helplessly. "Let me up! Let me go!"

"Why didn't you say who you were when you came down the stairs," Helen demanded. "You scared us half to death creeping around like that."

"I wasn't sure it was you," said the old man balefully. "I was just as scared as you were. Please put that thing down!" The Indian tucked his shirt tails into his pants and gazed mournfully at the scalpel that Pinky still held at his side.

"I was following him, you see?" he said. "Saw him slam the door down. Figured maybe somebody was in here, so I came down."

"Who were you following?" asked Helen.

"Why?" asked Pinky.

The Indian didn't answer. Inside the works of the Thurber machine lay a scrap of crumpled-up paper they hadn't noticed before with several letters of the alphabet typed on it.

"We better take this to the cops," said Pinky slyly.

"Wait a minute," said the Indian at the mention of the police. He sat heavily on the lowest of the cellar steps. "I don't know who he is," he mewled. "Swear to God. I was following him because he gives me this stuff. See? In the red bottles. Helps my leg. Good for the rheumatism. Met him last spring over at Sander's Ridge. Real nice to me. I told him about my leg, and next time I met him, he brought me one of the bottles. Three times that happened. Then last time he tried to charge me. I don't have no thirty bucks. I was mad, see? So I followed him, and now I found where he keeps it. Right there in those boxes." He pointed. "I don't want cops finding me," he pleaded. "They'll put me in the state old-folks' home."

"Who is he?" asked Helen.

"I don't know," said the Indian. "Just a guy. Ordinary-looking."

"Can you describe him so I can draw him?" asked Helen.

"Guess so," said the Indian. "Let's go up in the light. Cellar's damp. Brings on my pain again."

Helen had a pencil in her pocketbook but no paper. She ran to the closet at the back of the cellar. Surely there would be a piece of paper, a label of some kind. She grabbed a can of Dr. Buckland's Scotch Oats Essence and tried to pull off the wrapper, only to find it had been stuck on with a hundred-and-twenty-year-old version of Krazy Glue that smelled of fish. The candle, only half an inch long, now began to burn her fingers. She blew it out and stuffed it in her pocket. She reached wildly in among the shelves, over the lye soap in its slippery oil paper. There were ten large boxes in the back, under the Cuticura Anti-Pain Plasters. She opened one of the boxes and found tin upon tin about the size of pipe-tobacco cans. She picked them up one by one, but they were all sealed tightly with oil paper, except for the last. She breathed a sigh of great relief when the paper label slid off easily.

Helen ran up the stairs and out into the light. She flattened the thin paper on one of the smooth splints Pinky had found and sat next to the Indian on a fallen log.

"How old would you say he was?" he asked.

"Oh, young, young," said the Indian. "Then, of course, they all look young to me."

"Who's they?" asked Helen.

"Everybody," said the Indian. "I'm ninety-two."

When Helen had gotten the shape of the head, the ears, the hair, eyes, nose, and mouth all to the Indian's satisfaction, he rose and said, "You got 'im. That's him to a tee." His joints popped as he went down into the cellar again.

When he came back, he was wearing one of the great-coats. "Took all the red medicine," he said, grinning. "Put it all in the lining of this coat. Nice warm coat too." Then he limped off merrily, the hem of the coat dragging and bulging with bottles of laudanum, cure for all maladies and distempers of the human body. He turned and waved once and then clinked and clanked his way off into the fog-filled woods until they could hear him no more.

Chief Ryser was not in the mood. That, Helen and Pinky could tell the moment they were shown into his office. "Your folks have called," he said sternly to Helen. "Your aunt tried to find you up at the high school. She wanted us to put out a missing person on you two. I figured you'd turn up."

"Sir," said Pinky, "we found it." He put the crumpled scrap of paper with the Thurber type sample on Ryser's blotter. "We found the machine that was used to write the tip-off note about Stubby Atlas. Also the envelope that Helen's locket and the tape were in. It's in a basement up in the woods, off Route Six."

"And I have a sketch of the guy who was using it," said Helen. She caught Pinky's eye for a minute. They would not give the old Indian away. "We . . . I saw him for just a second."

Ryser looked at the type sample and the drawing blankly. "Well, you sure can draw," he said. He was trying to be kind, Helen knew. But his attention had died. "Frank!" he yelled. "File this and get these kids home before the girl's aunt has heart failure."

"Is that all?" Helen asked. "Aren't you going to go up and take fingerprints from the writing machine?"

"Honey," said Ryser, standing, leaning on his arms on the desk and shrugging his massive shoulders, "I told you before and I'll tell you again—" but he was interrupted.

"Where'd you get this, kids?" asked the sergeant at his side. "Where did you find this piece of paper?" He had turned Helen's drawing over and placed it, back up, on Ryser's desk.

Ryser scowled, put on his glasses, and read it. The color drained right out of his face and then right back in, until the tiny veins in his cheeks went magenta. "Where?" he asked.

"In the closet at the back of the old cellar," said Helen.

"Was it wrapped around a container?" snapped Ryser. "Was the container full and heavy? Were there other containers?"

"I don't know," answered Helen. "It was so dark. I couldn't see. There . . . yes, there were lots of them. Little tins like pipe tobacco comes in. They were full, all right. They'd never been unpacked. I pried open the carton myself."

Ryser turned to the sergeant. "Get on the horn," he said. "Call the lab. See if you can talk to the head, what's his name? Feinberg. Find out how long this stuff lasts. How long is it potent?"

Pinky had meanwhile taken the wrapper off Ryser's desk. He handed it to Helen without a word. She turned the paper so that she could read the fancy lettering. On it was printed:

PURE MORPHINE — 100% PURE

"Okay," said Ryser. He pointed his finger at Helen and kept it pointed. "How many cans of this stuff was in the cellar?"

Helen closed her eyes. She wanted to get it just right. She pictured herself in slow motion, struggling with the label of the Scotch oats cannister. Reaching over the lye soaps. Prying off the top of the carton. Reaching in. "At least twenty in the carton I opened," she said. "The carton was filled with sawdust. All the other cans were wrapped up tight in heavy oily paper. This was the only one that didn't have the oily paper on it. There were several stacks of cartons. All identical. I took this can from the top box on the left-hand stack. The cellar is very neat and orderly. Everything of one kind is kept together. I'd guess there were twenty cans to a carton and twelve cartons. Maybe ten cartons."

"Were the cans that you picked up heavy? All of them? Were they full?"

"Yes," said Helen.

The sergeant returned. "I talked to Feinberg," he said. "He talked to somebody up at Harvard. If the stuff is sealed tight and kept in a cool, dark place, it might last forever. Apparently somebody out in Ohio found an old bottle two years ago. Something called laudanum. Had it tested. The opium and alcohol were even more potent than they'd expected. It had aged like good wine."

"Then this morphine could still be converted to heroin," Ryser said, seeming dazed.

The sergeant shrugged. "Why not?" he said. "Converting it is easy for anybody with a hot plate and some liquid ether. The thing is, it's the morphine *itself* that's the gold. Converted or not, it's worth a mint and a half. If there's two hundred cans of morphine there—my God—I can't—I can't even begin to figure what that'd be worth on the street."

The fog had lifted and the rain had started again. Helen and Pinky each sat on the back seat of an enormous Harley-Davidson motorcycle, behind an enormous policeman. They tore through the peaceful woods with terrifying, ear-splitting noise and speed.

Helen wished she could talk about her tangled, rushing thoughts to Pinky. Around her policeman's huge blue back she could just see Pinky. He was up ahead on the first motorcycle, giving directions back to Lucy's basement. She pictured Pinky, laughing in his ironic way. "With our luck," he would say, "the typewriter will be clean of prints and the stuff in the cans will be gone by the time we get back there."

It was.

THIRTEEN

Helen's father talked to her in a voice he usually saved for water polluters. "Liar!" he said for the tenth time.

Helen sat on her bed, her father in a chair. She had been banished to her bedroom for an unspecified length of time the moment Chief Ryser had left the house with a silent, raging Pinky in tow.

"Dad," said Helen, trying to keep her voice steady, "the cans were full. I felt them. They were heavy."

"They were empty. The police went through every morphine cannister in those cartons, and every single one of them was *empty*."

"Dad, please. Please listen. I picked up all the cans in the carton I opened. They were sealed in an oily paper, all except for one, and they were all full. When the cops came back, every single can was empty, and the oily paper wrappings were gone. Somebody was there after Pinky and I left. By the time we got out of the police station, he would have had at least an hour and a half."

"The cartons were covered with dust," said her father. "The cops said they hadn't been touched in a hundred years."

"There was dust in every corner of that cellar, Dad. All he had to do was take handfuls of it and spread it on the boxes and cans."

"Can't you admit to a mistake?" asked her father. "Causing endless trouble and wasting the police's time. Embarrassing Aunt Stella and me. Can't you even do that?"

Helen wondered if he was softening slightly. He was saying mistake instead of lie. "It wasn't a mistake," she answered heatedly.

"Then it's a lie," said her father with even more heat. "It's a lie just like the lie you trumped up with your boyfriend. Said you were going up to school to the *Whaler,* didn't you? But you headed out to the woods. Had it all cooked up with him ahead of time, didn't you?"

"No, no, no, Dad. Pinky did invent that story, but we were halfway to the woods before I knew."

"You could have turned around!"

"No, I couldn't. You don't understand, Dad."

"You bet I don't. I understand my daughter's a liar. That's what I understand."

"You!" said Helen, her temper edging out despair. "You sitting down in the living room with Chief Ryser

half an hour ago! Not listening to Pinky or me. Just agreeing with him because he's a man. A man in a uniform.
You'd go along with anything any other man says. Being
one of the boys. That's all you care about!"

"That hurt," said her father.

"Well, you've hurt *me*!"

After he left, Helen sat alone on her bed. She did not
cry with the rage and fear that were boiling up inside her
but coolly took the morphine label and pinned it drawing
side out on the wall over her desk. She stared at the face.
The face stared at her. It was a good drawing. Something
told her she knew who it was. She struggled to make sense
of it, but he remained hidden behind just the wrong eyes,
mouth, and hair, like the dark side of a half-moon.

"Who are you?" she asked. "How do you plan to get
me? Are you going to get Pinky too?" *Innocent, careless
Pinky,* she thought. All the time that the Indian had been
describing the face she was drawing, someone had lain
hidden in the fog listening. He'd gone into the cellar after
they'd left, cleaned the prints off the Thurber, taken away
every grain in every can of morphine, and disappeared.
But now he knew she hadn't been good, hadn't watched
out. She put her hands over her eyes.

Aunt Stella knocked tentatively on the door. She'd
brought up a portion of tuna fish casserole on one of her
best Spode plates. "You have to eat," she said when Helen
showed no inclination to do so.

"Later, please, Aunt Stella," said Helen. "I'm doing my
homework."

When Aunt Stella left the room, for some reason tiptoeing as if not to disturb a sick patient, Helen shoved the plate of tuna fish away, against the little Hummel figurine that still stood, chipped staff in hand, on her desk top.

Her father came in to say good night. He looked at the untouched food. "Sweet Pea," he began, but everything that had welled up inside Helen surged out of her. She dropped her head on her cradled arms and cried as desperately as a mother who'd lost a child.

"I brought you some warm milk with nutmeg on it," he said. "Please, babe. I know it's hard to be a teenager. Your body goes through a lot of changes. Things'll seem better in the morning. Please drink the milk. It'll do you good."

"Go away," said Helen. "Please just go away with your milk and your teenage body changes!"

Helen did not lift her head until the house had long been still. Deep, regular snores came from her father's bedroom. Aunt Stella's bedroom was always deathly quiet, for Aunt Stella slept as deeply as a sunken ship.

There was nothing to say to Pinky, even if she summoned up the courage to call him. He would be at the motel desk tonight. Saturday was the Seafarer's busiest night. There was nothing she could tell him that he wouldn't have worked out in his own head already. All their hard work. All their disappointments and dead ends overcome, and what was left? She had hurt her father terribly, and he had hurt her. What was said could not be unsaid. Beyond was a desert of nothingness because she was afraid that *he,* whoever he was, would climb up the rose trellis and strangle her in her sleep—or her eyes . . . her eyes . . .

She stared at the face in her drawing again. Without the right shape and nose and mouth it meant nothing. Its expression was as passive as the Hummel figurine's. *Dear God, where are you tonight?* she asked miserably. But the only answer was the pouring, unrelenting rain.

That's it, she decided. It was like having a rare illness that no one understood. She would have to spend years watching, listening, never concentrating for a minute on anything more than whether there were enough people around to keep her safe. And she would worry about Pinky, whom she'd dragged into this. Free Pinky, cocksure and unafraid. She tore the drawing down from the wall and shoved it into her wastebasket. For good measure she picked up the Hummel figurine and all the bottled-up fury came out again and she pitched it like a fast ball across the room. It bounced against the wall and began to play.

"Oh, shut up!" Helen growled, and she reached for it to stop the key. Once more her breathing came short, and she felt for the floor, as if the house and room itself were about to dissolve. After the music box had run through its tune, she wound it up again and replayed it to make sure. It wasn't necessary. "The Happy Wanderer" was printed on the underside of the figurine.

Helen snatched the drawing from the wastebasket and flattened it out on her desk. She watched as the slightly distorted features grew together and became a face she knew well. There was pure joy in her voice when she said, *"I'm going to get you first."*

Helen pulled on her winter parka. Holding the front of it open, she drew the telephone in against herself, muffling the sound of the dial. When a sleepy Pinky answered "Seafarer," she said only one thing. "Come *now*!"

Twenty minutes went by with Helen waiting, unmoving, gazing through the bay window of the darkened living room at the watery street. At last across the road there were two blinks from the weak flashlight. She let herself out the kitchen way, closing the door painfully slowly. She ran around the front of the house, splashed across the puddles, and jumped on the back of Pinky's motorbike.

"What? Where?" he asked desperately. "I had a terrible time getting out. I made my sister take the desk. I had to promise her ten things to make her do it."

On the way Helen blessed the rain for keeping the streets clear of traffic. They had never gone downtown before on the motorbike. If the police picked them up . . . She didn't want to think what would happen if the police picked them up. Between snatches of explanation into Pinky's ear she kept a sharp watch out for patrol cars. *It would be our luck,* she told herself, *to get stopped now.* Pinky made a sudden right turn, and she nearly fell off the bike. "What was that?" she asked, peering back into the downpour.

"Squad car," he said, "cooping."

He drove into a deserted parking lot in the middle of town. They walked, not letting go of each other's hands.

The fire escape on the corner building zigzagged up five stories. One corner of the fifth floor was lighted. The rain beat down like a drum tattoo on the garbage cans in the alley and hid the noise as Pinky jumped like a basketball player and pulled down the squeaky iron ladder. Up the open gridwork steps they crept. For three or four minutes they watched him behind the iron bars and through a skewed blind of Perry and Crowe's supply-room window.

Helen whispered, "Stubby Atlas knew what he was doing after all. He knew what was in those trucks."

Barry worked steadily by the light of a single chrome lamp. The work table was covered with different Hummel figurines. The music boxes had been removed, and into the cavities where the music boxes went he sifted small amounts of white powder with a tiny silver scoop. Then he plastered gold Perry and Crowe gift stickers over the openings, placed the Hummel figurines in Perry and Crowe gift boxes, and addressed the label on each box after consulting a small red book.

After addressing each box he dropped it into a hopper marked *UPS Truck* and started in on the next. From time to time he wound up one of the little music box workings and whistled along with it.

Pinky did not stay. He went off down the stairs of the fire escape. He was gone for what seemed to Helen like an hour, and then suddenly he was back at her side, panting.

"Did you call the police?" Helen asked.

Pinky shook his head. "I called Brzostoski," he said. "He called the cops. Told them there was a robbery in progress, fifth floor Perry and Crowe. Not to run the sirens."

Barry's body stiffened and then sagged when he saw the policeman. The officer hesitated. "Robbery in progress?"

he asked, hand on his revolver. Pinky wrenched open the window and was in the room, pointing to a plastic bag of white powder at Barry's side. "Look at it!" Pinky yelled. "Come over here and look at what's in this bag and what he's putting into those little music boxes!"

"You don't have a warrant to come in here," Barry snarled. "You need a search warrant!" He got up and placed a chair between himself and Pinky, for some reason.

Dear God, Helen prayed silently, *please don't make them need a search warrant!* The policeman strolled thoughtfully over to a green garbage bag that lay under the table full of Hummel figurines. Three other policemen walked quietly in through the door and watched him. The first officer ran his fingers through the powdery white substance and touched one to his tongue.

"You need a *search warrant!*" Barry screamed.

"Shipping Johnson's baby powder out in these things?" asked the officer.

Soon there were ten other policemen in the room. One was Frank, Ryser's chief deputy. He looked at Pinky first, then Helen, and then at Barry's array of materials. He picked up the little red book. "Atlas's," he said. "Atlas's father's book with the addresses of all his drug dealer pals." He shook his head. "How?" he asked them. "How did you find this. How?"

When Helen had no answer but a smile he turned to Barry. "And who the devil are you?" he asked.

"I don't have to tell you that," Barry snarled. "My constitutional rights—"

"Shut up, Barry," said Pinky. "His name is Barry de

Wolf," Pinky went on. "Senior at New Bedford Regional. Big Shot. Birdwatcher. That's probably how he found the cellar in the first place. Poking around the woods after blue jays."

"Yeah?" said the policeman edging toward Barry. He picked up the little red book. "And how did you find this? Birdwatching too?" He waved the book in front of Barry before slipping it into his pocket. "A lot of interesting names and addresses in this book, de Wolf. Aren't there? We're going to put you and a lot of Chet Malinka's good buddies out of business. How did you get it?"

Barry spat out, "My constitutional rights are being—"

"Okay!" said the policeman, grinning and holding up a deferential hand.

"He worked for Perry and Crowe this summer. Still does," said Pinky casually. "He lifted it off Stubby, probably."

"The moron lost it," Barry snarled. "I never stole anything in my life."

The policeman had dropped his hand to his side. He looked again at one of the Hummel figurines. "So Stubby knew what he was doing after all," he said slowly. "He did want to rob the china and glass shipments. Sure he did. He could feed his habit and go into business on the side with what was in these little statues. You," he said, pointing vaguely in Barry's direction, "you found the dope in the cellar. All you needed was an outlet, some way to sell it without getting your hands dirty on the street. Must have been like a gift dropped from heaven when Stubby Atlas showed up for work with his dad's addresses in his back pocket. Tell me, why does a boy with your brains and imagination go out and ruin his life like this? You're not a minor, de Wolf. You'll get at least twenty years, you know."

Barry was led out by two policemen. Several more hovered over Pinky and Helen asking twenty different questions at once. Pinky began with Uncle Max. Helen followed with Lucy.

"Do you two have any idea how much this stuff is worth?" was the question asked most. A reporter in a dirty trenchcoat came in. Then another. "Can we get you anything?" they were asked again and again.

"Yes," said Helen at last. "Call my dad."

Ryser was dressed in old corduroys and a plaid shirt. Like all the others he looked into the plastic bag and ran his fingers through the powder and tasted it. He plodded over to Helen and Pinky. "As I've always said," he began, coughing sheepishly, "the hardest thing about growing up is learning to admit you've made a mistake." He looked down at his feet and shook his head in disbelief. "Nothing more I can say. Nothing I can do to thank you," he added. Then he beckoned and called over two of the policemen by name. He unpinned the badge from each man's shirt front and solemnly pinned them onto Helen's soaking parka and Pinky's still-dripping rain slicker, like medals.

The shiny silver badges were the first things that Helen's father saw.

Helen rode home, sitting between her father and Pinky in the front seat. The motorbike took up the whole of the back of the station wagon. On one side she held Pinky's hand. On the other she fell asleep against her father's shoulder.

Helen woke enough to walk into the house under her own steam. Aunt Stella waited in a dressing gown. She said only "Shhhh!" her finger against her lips when Helen passed by. Her father pulled off her wet parka and led her to her bed, covering her with her quilt and kissing her as softly as a butterfly brushing her forehead with its wing.

Helen woke up hours later, in damp, uncomfortable clothes with a hard lump under one thigh. She undressed and put on her nightgown. In the pocket of her jeans she discovered the candle end she'd saved from Lucy's cellar. She put it in a pin dish right in front of the ebony-framed portrait of Lucy and Lorenzo.

She lit the little candle end and watched as the wick took and the flame glowed. Next to the portrait was the older Lucy, the one in the Valdosta newspaper. *Should I write your story or not?* she asked herself.

Out of Lucy's magnificent black eyes she tried to pry a signal. The signal was there. It came from across the divide of mortal time, from beyond the planets in the land of the dead. But whether the answer was yes or no, Helen couldn't tell.

It's up to me, isn't it? she said slowly to herself. She looked back at the picture of Lucy and Lorenzo that Mrs. Fairchild had pressed into her hands, her eyes, like the younger Lucy's, filled with trust.

Enough wrong has been done, and enough right too, Helen decided. She pinched out the candle. Someone else could write the story.